MY YEAR IN PARIS
WITH GERTRUDE STEIN

By the same author

Ophelia and the Great Idea
Beautiful Mutants
Swallowing Geography
The Unloved
Diary of a Steak
Billy & Girl
Pillow Talk in Europe and Other Places
Swimming Home
Black Vodka
Things I Don't Want to Know
Hot Milk
The Cost of Living
The Man Who Saw Everything
Real Estate
August Blue

MY YEAR IN PARIS WITH GERTRUDE STEIN

A Fiction

Deborah Levy

HAMISH HAMILTON
an imprint of
PENGUIN BOOKS

HAMISH HAMILTON

UK | USA | Canada | Ireland | Australia
India | New Zealand | South Africa

Hamish Hamilton is part of the Penguin Random House group of companies whose addresses can be found at global.penguinrandomhouse.com

Penguin Random House UK,
One Embassy Gardens, 8 Viaduct Gardens, London SW11 7BW

penguin.co.uk

First published 2026

001

Copyright © Deborah Levy, 2026

Extracts from *Lifting Belly* by Gertrude Stein,
reproduced by permission of Counterpoint Press

The moral right of the author has been asserted

Penguin Random House values and supports copyright. Copyright fuels creativity, encourages diverse voices, promotes freedom of expression and supports a vibrant culture. Thank you for purchasing an authorized edition of this book and for respecting intellectual property laws by not reproducing, scanning or distributing any part of it by any means without permission. You are supporting authors and enabling Penguin Random House to continue to publish books for everyone. No part of this book may be used or reproduced in any manner for the purpose of training artificial intelligence technologies or systems. In accordance with Article 4(3) of the DSM Directive 2019/790, Penguin Random House expressly reserves this work from the text and data mining exception

Set in 14.25/18.75pt Fournier MT Pro
Typeset by Six Red Marbles UK, Thetford, Norfolk
Printed and bound in Great Britain by Clays Ltd, Elcograf S.p.A.

The authorized representative in the EEA is Penguin Random House Ireland,
Morrison Chambers, 32 Nassau Street, Dublin D02 YH68

A CIP catalogue record for this book is available from the British Library

ISBN: 978–0–241–45780–1

Penguin Random House is committed to a sustainable future
for our business, our readers and our planet. This book is made from
Forest Stewardship Council® certified paper.

'About six weeks ago Gertrude Stein said, it does not look to me as if you were ever going to write that autobiography. You know what I am going to do. I am going to write it for you. I am going to write it as simply as Defoe did the autobiography of Robinson Crusoe. And she has and this is it.'

The Autobiography of Alice B. Toklas (1933) by Gertrude Stein

'It is a joy to be hidden and a disaster not to be found'

Playing and Reality (1971) by D. W. Winnicott

I

PARIS. NOVEMBER 2024

Eva called to say she had lost it.

She meant her cat who had gone missing. Eva was my new friend in Paris. We liked not knowing much about each other because there was so much to find out. When I left Paris for a month at the end of July, she had sent a postcard to my London address.

Summer kisses from me and it.

I had to think about who it was but then remembered it was the name of her cat. On the other side of the card Eva had drawn it in a tracksuit and lime-green running shoes holding a flaming torch in the 2024 Paris

Olympics. The postcard was addressed to my first name only.

We went through all the possibilities of where it might have got to and knocked on the door of every neighbour in her road. Eva lived in a studio in the Rue des Trois Portes, a two-minute walk to the Seine and the Notre-Dame cathedral of Paris. Before it disappeared, she kept her front door ajar on a chain so that no one could barge in when her cat padded down the stairs to the courtyard. Her husband lived in Seattle, America. She had lost him. The cat. It slept on her bed and Eva said its purring sounds were her equivalent of the Christmas lights that would soon be threaded through the trees in our neighbourhood. A week before it went missing, our mutual friend, Fanny, who worked in finance, had renamed Eva's cat Bob. Fanny wore a belt strapped across her narrow hips, her eyes clear and bright, jewels on her nails, a cigarette often tucked into her belt.

'I'm sorry, Eva,' Fanny said. 'It is doing my head in. From now on it is Bob. We know where we are with Bob.'

'Where are we then?' Eva wanted to know.

'I don't exactly know,' she replied. 'In France Bob would be Rob.'

Fanny seemed barely with us. She was living some kind of parallel life in the erotic altitudes with her most cherished lover, Lucia, one of her three lovers in the month of November. She was the only one in our friendship group who was French. Every day Fanny reminded me to ride my bicycle on the right-hand side of the road, not on the left, also to buy a helmet because I rode on those e-bikes that are hired on a phone. On behalf of her clients, Fanny was keeping a close eye on the American elections which were to take place on 5 November 2024.

Eva had trimmed her fringe in the mirror that morning. It was straight, symmetrical, just above her eyebrows. She had inherited her Spanish mother's black hair and her Danish father's blue eyes. Everyone went Awww when they looked into Eva's eyes. She had discovered her favourite cologne (notes of thyme and cedar wood) in a hardware shop on the Rue des

Écoles, laid out in its tall retro bottle on the counter alongside limescale remover, cutlery sets and tubes of tile cement. Fanny believes that Eva's blue eyes have to fight fight fight with the world's fantasy of endless girlhood and submission, but she's not sure the industrial cologne is going to help her in this endeavour – though it will see off mosquitoes.

I call her Eva the Fifth because she speaks five languages: Danish, Spanish, French, German and English. She regrets her German is not so fluent, even though she studied at a leading art school in Berlin, so insists I change her title to Eva the Fourth.

As far as Eva was concerned her cat was God in every language.

Bob was love. Black fur. White belly, white paws. Right ear smaller than the left. Much smaller. The size of the smallest human toe. Fanny, who was raised Catholic, suggested that God is a judging presence and Bob was not, but Eva confirmed that her cat definitely judged her.

The whole drama, which was a tragedy for

Eva, was a relief from writing my essay on Gertrude Stein, about whom I knew too much and nothing at all. Stein had put so much in my way. In the way of understanding. She didn't believe in it. Sometimes, when I read her baffling and beguiling writing I wanted to smack it in the chops. She longed for readers to find her, yet there was a part of her that could not bear to be found. She was ashamed of her bestselling autobiography because it was so understandable. When I look at photographs of her, I cannot get into her eyes. Sometimes I had to remind myself of the basic facts, so lost was I in the swirl of information about her.

Gertrude Stein was born in 1874, Allegheny, Pennsylvania, America. Daughter of German Jewish immigrants. Her father, Daniel Stein, born in Bavaria, arrived in America in 1841 at the age of eighteen to start a clothing business with his brother Solomon. Her mother, Amelia Keyser, daughter of earlier immigrants from Bavaria, was born in America. Daniel would become a wealthy businessman. His youngest child, Gertrude Stein, would become a legend, a leading figure of literary modernism, possibly the only female avant-garde writer in the world to have her name up in lights in Times Square. Writer of novels, plays, poetry, essays, libretti, and collector of the most daring art of the early twentieth century, she also wrote 'word portraits' which she hoped resembled the radical visions of Cézanne, Matisse and Picasso. She would be photographed by Man Ray and Cecil Beaton, Picasso would paint her portrait, she would live in France from the age of twenty-nine and die there at the age of seventy-two. Yet Gertrude Stein struggled to be published and only stepped into fame and gloire when she was nearly sixty. She was good friends with a collaborator in the Vichy regime during World War II. Ernest Hemingway described her as having 'immigrant hair'.

I had lost it. Who was Gertrude Stein?

Immigrant hair. What do words mean?

*

Gertrude Stein deliberately reduced her vocabulary as a writer. She did not want to work from a vast menu of words. Her future wife, Alice B., would cook up a vast menu of dishes instead, including a soufflé made with candied violets.

'You are of course never yourself.' This is a quote from Gertrude Stein's Everybody's Autobiography, and I think it meant something to Eva. It meant something to me. Perhaps that is what modernity is all about. Not being yourself. Is that a desirable way to live? Or is it the only way to live? How do we put ourselves together? Stein, the daughter of immigrants, was obsessed with what she called 'composition'.

Composition from the Latin componere, meaning 'to put together', or 'to bring all the parts together'.

Meanwhile, Eva, who was born in Copenhagen, continued searching for it who was now Bob and not Rob while November rain fell on the tall yellow cranes restoring Notre-Dame. Fanny and I wondered about Eva's absent husband, but she made it clear she was not hospitable to prying and poking for information. We knew he was from Aberdeen and his name was Hamish. He was a carpenter on film sets, based in Seattle but travelling to wherever work took him. Eva was working on a graphic novel in Paris. They had not seen each other for a year and FaceTimed once a week. Eva usually had her cat on her lap when they spoke. Fanny, who was sometimes present for these calls – she said Eva's Wi-Fi was faster than her own – told me that most of their conversation was about the cat. It was as if Eva and Hamish spoke about their own situation through Bob.

I suggested to Fanny this might be why her cat ran away. It had not consented to be a participant in their marriage, or to fill in the gaps in their communication, or to listen to their problems.

'Yes,' Fanny agreed, 'Bob was not equipped to help them negotiate their differences.' While rain fell on the pigeons in Rue Maître Albert, an old narrow road in the 5th arrondissement, I noticed we had started referring to Bob in the past tense. Gertrude Stein wrote in the continuous present tense. Eva's quest to find her cat alive and living in the now meant Fanny and I tried to only use the continuous present tense when we mentioned Bob in Eva's presence.

'If I don't find it I might as well jump into the Seine,' Eva said.

I noticed she had placed a persimmon fruit to ripen on the ledge of her window. She told me she was looking forward to tasting it. That was a good sign. Eva lived on the sixth floor of her building.

2

Meanwhile, bombs are falling through the twenty-first century upon the living and the soon-to-be dead. They all have names and surnames in our own century, in the month of November. We are on our screens all the time, scrolling, scrolling, scrolling through the various wars in the twenty-fourth year of the twenty-first century. Gertrude Stein lived through two world wars and wrote a memoir, titled Wars I Have Seen, published in 1945. She did not see either of these wars on a screen. Advertisements for vitamins, automobiles and life insurance interrupted news of the wars I was watching on the screen in my hand, also the screech of one solitary parakeet perched in a tree in the courtyard, the bells of

Notre-Dame nearby, rain pelting down on the skylight window above my bed, the sound of coffee boiling in the espresso pot on the gas hob and the gasping sounds I made internally at the violence on my screen.

3

I am walking through the hundred and ten acres of Père Lachaise cemetery in the 20th arrondissement to find the grave of Gertrude Stein. Here in the wind and rain I see the dead buried in my mind, lit up, lit up with life, vanity, suffering and fame. I know what a few of them looked like from photographs and paintings, the various attitudes in their eyes and their various talents. Oscar Wilde, Edith Piaf, Chopin, Proust, Apollinaire, Georges Perec, Colette, Modigliani are all buried here.

As it happens, I know about Modigliani's various paintings of his friend, the artist Chaïm Soutine, their friendship in Paris during World War I, the way he lit Chaïm's eyes with a dot of paint the size of a pinhead. This gave him purpose and will. Chaïm Soutine, born in Smilovitchi (present-day Belarus), so young, battered, poor and hopeful when he arrived in Paris to chance his luck as an artist. Sometimes he was homeless and hungry. A doctor had to remove a nest of bedbugs from his ear. These two refugee painters did not get conscripted in 1914. How fortunate they were to have the gracious Marie Vassilieff from Russia, student of Matisse, turn her Montparnasse studio into a canteen for artists who were struggling in the war. It was a time of wounding and killing so no one was buying their work.

Marie Vassilieff also hosted a banquet for Georges Braque, the co-founder of cubism, when he returned to Paris, part of his head shattered with shrapnel. When Modigliani arrived at this banquet, drunk, looking for a fight, she lifted her arms and pushed him down the stairs. Then she carved the chicken.

Apollinaire was also wounded in the war, stationed in the mud of the trenches of Champagne. What else are wars for except wounding? What else are words for except to press on a wound? He returned to Paris in 1916 with a head injury and would only live eighteen years into the twentieth century. Guillaume Apollinaire is my craziest poet muse. He died from influenza in 1918, aged thirty-eight, along with millions of other people also struck down by this strangely undocumented pandemic rampaging through Europe. Muses are a projection, a delusion without needs or biography (what do we know about the families of female muses?), but I definitely understand he was a real man and did not exist just to inspire me. He was a major poet, a gourmand, a critic, intellectual and writer of erotic letters from the deepest mud of the trenches, also inventor of the word surrealism. Picasso used to joke that Apollinaire, who never met his Italian father, was the son of the pope. Gertrude Stein enjoyed Apollinaire's exuberance, admired his agile mind and avant-garde sensibility. They were good friends. He described the shattering of a bullet as 'flowering mimosa', but perhaps not the bullet that shattered his own skull.

In January my studio in Paris will be full of

mimosa. I will hang a bunch on my front door to welcome my new friends in Paris, who are also strangers, to my table.

I know a few things about Oscar Wilde. Oscar Fingal O'Fflahertie Wills Wilde from Dublin. He had just published The Ballad of Reading Gaol when he set foot in Paris in 1898. Stein would arrive five years later, by which time he would be dead. When he eventually found the hotel room in which he died, on the Rue des Beaux Arts, he ate the same lunch every day, a lamb chop and two boiled eggs. Fortunately, he drank four bottles of brandy a week to gentle the pain of the injustice that broke him. When he was young, he wore a stylish velvet cape, his hair long and free. Dying and high on morphine he converted to Catholicism. The statue on his grave, a winged sphinx with sandstone penis and testicles, crowned with a tiara, was made by American artist Jacob Epstein. When he arrived at Père Lachaise to put the finishing touches to this sculpture, he discovered it was surrounded by the gendarmerie. The tomb was 'under arrest' and the testicles on the statue had been covered by plaster 'to protect public decency'.

An epitaph in Wilde's own words is carved into the stone on the back of the tomb:

And alien tears will fill for him
Pity's long-broken urn
For his mourners will be outcast men
And outcasts always mourn.
      The Ballad of Reading Gaol (1904)

Oscar Wilde's grave is covered in lipstick kisses. No one has kissed Proust's grave. Made from sterner material, grey marble, it does not invite the kisses of strangers. Proust is embraced in the soil of his own country. Oscar Wilde has a martyred body and Marcel Proust has a private body.

I know some things about Gertrude Stein's body, too. When she was in her twenties it would be bent over a microscope.

Stein was going to devote eight years of her life to scientific investigation, first at Radcliffe

College in 1893 when she was nineteen, now Harvard, and then four years at Johns Hopkins in Baltimore. As a medical student at Johns Hopkins, Stein worked a few hours each day in the pathology lab to research the development of the human brain in the embryo. There she is. A future pioneer of the modernist movement wearing a blouse with large puffed sleeves and a bell-shaped skirt stiffened at the hem with a lining of horsehair. Sitting at her desk in the laboratory staring down a microscope, one of the early female students at Hopkins taking a medical degree. She will eventually stare at modern art instead and try to work out how it is put together. She had no idea how to put herself together.

Her thick hair is piled on top of her head in a chaotic bun. A few decades later she is going to ask her wife, Alice B. Toklas, to cut it all off. Out come the pins. Where are the scissors?

And where is James Joyce? Stein was furious that Ulysses was published before her own novel, The Making of Americans. He is buried with his family in Zurich, along with his two main phobias, thunder and dogs.

Gertrude and Alice B. loved their two giant white poodles, Basket 1 and his successor, Basket 2, also their little dog Pepe. Gertrude would listen to the rhythm of Basket's tongue lapping water from a bowl and claim it helped her understand the difference between writing sentences and writing paragraphs. She considered paragraphs to be more emotional than sentences. The various Baskets literally spoke in tongues to Gertrude Stein.

Alice B. liked to bath Basket 1 in sulphur water.

Looking at the map it's a twenty-five-minute walk to her grave.

What I am thinking as the wind blows my hair around is that Stein put her immense writing energies into making sure she was not understood. This is what interested me most about her writing. She did not believe it is worth having a conversation if everything is understandable.

Is this a desirable way to live? Or is it the only way to live?

'They ask me to tell why an author like myself can become popular. It is very easy everybody keeps saying and writing what anybody feels that they are understanding and so they get tired of that, anybody can get tired of anything everybody can get tired of something and so they do not know it but they get tired of feeling they are understanding and so they take pleasure in having something that they feel they are not understanding.'
  Everybody's Autobiography (1937) by Gertrude Stein

I am hiking in the rain in the hope that I might find it.
  What is it?
  Daring.
  Courage.

What did she want words to do and what did they do for her?

'It takes a lot of time to be a genius, you have to sit around so much doing nothing, really doing nothing.'
Everybody's Autobiography

I agree that everyone spends some of their time thinking without consciously thinking. Is that understandable? Does it matter?

Gertrude Stein worked in obscurity until the age of fifty-nine, when she wrote the best-selling Autobiography of Alice B. Toklas. She was lost to readers for decades. But I know she wanted to be found and Alice B. knew that as well. In the 1950s and '60s, poet Frank O'Hara found her and the Living Theatre found her. She was an American expatriate who had made a space for the American avant-garde in America to happen. But she was dead by then.

*

I had to keep reminding myself she was born in 1874.

Some of her titles were:

Tender Buttons: Objects, Food, Rooms

Have They Attacked Mary. He Giggled

A Book Concluding with As a Wife Has a Cow: A Love Story

A Village: Are You Ready Yet Not Yet: A Play in Four Acts

Lucy Church Amiably

Her wish to kill the nineteenth century still leaves an afterglow of radical resistance in our own century. How did she kill the nineteenth century? With her pen. After writing her more conventional early trio of novellas, Three Lives, she poked her pen under the bonnet of the nineteenth century and whipped it off. And then she set to work on the shawl.

In Jane Austen's novel Emma, written in 1815, Miss Bates (described wittily by Austen as 'a great talker upon little matters') insists that her mother wear a shawl when she goes visiting. After all, their low-cut Regency dresses were light and flimsy, and England, with its endless talk about little matters, was cold, riddled with class antagonisms, tea rituals and the necessity of securing a husband, which was a big economic matter.

'I made her take her shawl—for the evenings are not warm—her large new shawl—Mrs. Dixon's wedding-present.—So kind of her to think of my mother! Bought at Weymouth, you know—Mr. Dixon's choice.'

Stein killed this nineteenth-century shawl in her collection of prose poems, Tender Buttons, published in 1914.

'A SHAWL.

A shawl is a hat and hurt and a red balloon and an under coat and a sizer a sizer of talks.'

'They were entering the hall. Mr. Knightley's eyes had preceded Miss Bates's in a glance at Jane. From Frank Churchill's face, where he thought he saw confusion suppressed or laughed away, he had involuntarily turned to hers; but she was indeed behind, and too busy with her shawl.'

    Emma

'A shawl is a wedding, a piece of wax a little build. A shawl.'

    Tender Buttons

Alice B. Toklas would have typed out these words just as I have done. Stein wrote by hand at night and left the pages for Alice B. to gather in the morning. Alice B. was in love with Gertrude, as excited to harvest her words as she was to harvest the radishes she later grew in the garden of their country home. Frankly, my life is being ruined by Gertrude. Is it respectful to refer to her as Gertrude? Picasso called Gertrude Stein by her first name. She is often referred to as Miss Stein in The Autobiography of Alice B. Toklas. I could be at home reflecting on all of this, or being a genius and doing nothing at all. It is raining hard now in Père Lachaise, my trainers are soaked, I am working too hard for her. I'm not sure she worked that hard for me. If Ernest Hemingway, who was her friend in Paris and she his mentor, is to be believed, she never revised a draft. I don't believe him.

What do we have to lose to become modern?

She had to lose her corset. The hourglass figure. It was Miss Stein's pleasure to lift up her fork and knife and saw through a five-inch steak. Only men were allowed to possess appetite, but she had no desire to make herself smaller to please men.

And she did lose it. The corset. The hourglass was smashed because she was ahead of her time.

The experimental pull of Stein's writing across the twentieth century was made with her training in early psychology. Her writing can mostly be read through her enchantment with the vision of her tutor at Radcliffe College, the psychologist and philosopher William James – the 'movement of thoughts and words endlessly the same and endlessly different'.

That was the beginning of Stein finding something like a technique. The visual language of cubism offered her some strategies too. Early psychology and cubism. This is already an exciting mix of influences for a writer. The language of her new century, the twentieth century, came to her through being the fifth and youngest child of German Jewish immigrants. As a child, Stein spoke German and English at home. Secrets would have been whispered by adults in the language less familiar to the children. I thought about the Stein parents speaking secrets or arguing with each other in German when the five children were in bed. They probably did not want to be understood by the children. The French child psychoanalyst Françoise Dolto, born in 1908, saw a child as 'entirely language in their being'. Is it true the entire being of a child is made from language? Françoise Dolto was therapist to the French writer Georges Perec when he ran away from school at the age of twelve. His mother had been murdered in Auschwitz when he was seven.

'It is on a day like this one, a little later, a little earlier, that you discover without surprise, that something is wrong, that, without mincing words, you don't know how to live, that you will never know.'

A Man Asleep (1967) by Georges Perec

Perec's ashes are held in the columbarium of Père Lachaise, the row of cloisters in which the ashes of various dead are contained, Division 87, box 382. His mother had arrived in Paris from Warsaw in the 1920s when she was seven. She worked as a hairdresser and then in a watch-making factory. Perec's Polish father had many jobs: delivery driver, turner, moulder. So then, bourgeois Stein and working-class Perec were both born to foreign, Jewish parents, German and Polish. Perec regarded himself as French. Stein regarded herself as American.

Stein is buried in Division 94.

*

The experimental pull of Stein's language came to her from learning how to talk about visual art and her friendship with Picasso and from being queer. It came from escaping the tyranny of her father, who had died when she was seventeen. Virginia Woolf in 1928 wrote of the death of her own demanding father, 'His life would have entirely ended mine. What would have happened? No writing, no books; – inconceivable.'

With all of this, Stein made a language quite different from her own reading, the books she devoured in her late teens. Shakespeare, Richardson, Wordsworth, Trollope, Browning, Swift, Defoe, Keats, Byron.

She would meet the woman she considered to be her wife in 1907. It would be love at first sight for Alice B. Toklas. Originally from San Francisco, chain-smoker with a taste for expensive gloves, she would stuff lettuce leaves with sweetbreads and truffles cooked in sherry for her beloved, edit her work, help Gertrude self-publish her work and find time to sauté one hundred frog legs in butter and cream.

*

As it happens, Stein and her siblings had a modest trust fund from their deceased father's cable car business in San Francisco. Her older brother Michael Stein looked after their stocks and shares and rental income from various properties he purchased in San Francisco. She would receive a monthly allowance, never have to work or endure being sexually available to a husband in return for his guardianship. Instead she would support Alice B., who described their erotic life as 'gathering wild violets'.

What I am thinking as the wind blows my hair around and rain soaks my shoes is that I'm going home without finding her grave. Yes, I am going to find the exit. Earlier that morning I had queued up at my local boulangerie for a particular baguette that is charred at each end, cut it in half and inserted into it a slab of oozing Brie. Its salty grey rind, like ash, had cracked from the sheer life force of this fast-flowing river of cheese. If the rind was the frame, this Brie like Gertrude Stein had burst through it. My cheeks stinging in the wind, the trees dripping,

I unwrapped the oozing baguette and devoured it there and then amongst the dead. The living have appetites. Desires. To drive us mad. To make us joyful. To make us cry. To lead us up the wrong path and down the right path. The dead have done all that. The dead who can no longer feel the rain had spent a lifetime creating themselves.

4

Creating herself. Creating themselves. The performance of it. The confusion of it. The pleasure of it. Gertrude Stein. Born in Allegheny, Pennsylvania, in 1874. Making a life. Making a life with love in it. Creating a body with no shame in it. Gertrude Stein did not fit the Victorian ideal of femininity and she knew it. She did not want it either. Creating a body of work. That no one else could have written. Collector of the most daring art of the early twentieth century. Cézanne. Picasso. Matisse. The 'outlaw' painters who were mocked and struggling at the time. Curating, at the age of twenty-nine, the first modern art gallery in Europe in the flat she rented with her brother in Paris. And then she set about finding herself a wife and separating from her brother, who had begun to undermine her writing. Making a home. Gertrude Stein and Alice B. Toklas. A home of their own. Surviving two world wars. She died of stomach cancer in the American Hospital of Paris in 1946, the city she made her 'home town'.

5

Fanny has just told me that her most cherished lover, Lucia, told her a cat drowned yesterday in the Canal Saint-Martin. Apparently, it had one ear smaller than the other. She would get more information; in the meanwhile I was to tell Eva that Fanny would be doing a raclette at her place tomorrow night. 'Don't say anything about the drowned cat,' Fanny insisted. And because I am from Britain, Fanny explained that Raclette is a semi-hard Alpine cheese known for its ability to melt. Yes, Raclette is promiscuous. It will melt for everyone. Right-wing, left-wing, it doesn't care. Fanny owned a raclette electrique, which comes with a grill and individual pans so that each person can melt their slice of cheese. She also suggested that I donate my fur hat to a charitable organization and swap my Gertrude Stein books for a guide to essential French grammar. She wondered if she should include mushrooms on the menu for the raclette? Fanny and her third lover in the month of November, Nicole, had gathered a good haul of mushrooms on a foraging expedition to Normandy. Sometimes I called her Fanny the Third. Fanny had brought some of these mushrooms over for Eva and me. We laid them out on a sheet of paper in Eva's studio, which had become our headquarters in Paris, but Eva wasn't convinced that more than six of them could be safely identified. The weird thing was that Nicole, who had made an omelette for herself with her share of the haul, had thrown up two hours later, but Fanny, who had also made an omelette for herself and her most cherished lover, Lucia, said they were both more than okay and so was Martine, the second lover, who finished up the ceps (the six mushrooms Eva could identify) in a dish she had created with cream, mustard and Parmesan. Fanny required a nourishing menu to support her vigorous sex life, but really she was in love with Lucia. Deeply in love. The frantic pace of her erotic assignments seemed to give her the edge professionally. Fanny's clients in the world of finance suddenly took investment risks they were not inclined to take. If she was persuasive with the more cautious of her clients, they did not understand that she was in a constant state of amorous flush. So far it had worked out for them, and for Fanny, who declared she despised her job. She often told Eva that she thought about capitalism in the same way Roland Barthes thought about language, 'it wounds or seduces me'. Fanny had long glossy chestnut hair which she sometimes wore in a high ponytail. Eva, who was very interested in my research on Stein, wondered if Fanny washed her hair in sulphur water, like the poodles, Basket 1 and Basket 2. Gertrude and Alice were totally sexed up too, but I think Alice B. washed the poodles in sulphur water to tame the odour of the dogs. Sometimes, when I was deep in thought about Gertrude Stein, my neighbour would step on to his balcony and stand in the cold weather almost naked, apart from a small towel draped across his hips. Perhaps he was looking for the parakeet in the tree in the courtyard?

6

Gertrude Stein wanted to kill the nineteenth century.

The twenty-first century seems to be killing itself.

7

When I told Eva that Gertrude Stein riffed on Descartes' first principle of philosophy, 'I think, therefore I am', with 'I am I because my little dog knows me', Eva wasn't that impressed.

'My cat doesn't know me any more. It is like an orphan now.'

After her cat went missing, I said, 'Eva, do you mind that we renamed it Bob?' She obviously did mind.

'I don't think it is too difficult to pronounce.'

There was something like tears in her eyes but she was upset about things even before she lost it. It was as if by renaming her cat it had become lost twice. After a while Eva let us refer to her cat as Bob, as if she was making things easier for us.

*

I suppose Bob was more like realism.

I felt relieved and slightly soiled at not being able to cope with it.

'My writing is clear as mud, but mud settles and clear streams run on and disappear.'
    Everybody's Autobiography

I wanted my essay to be a clear stream, but there was so much going on. A lost cat, Eva's missing husband, the vast menu of Fanny's erotic conquests, finding my way around Paris, the temptation to put down Stein's writing and read Georges Simenon instead. The streams were flowing through the nineteenth century into the twenty-first and all over the place. Were they streams of consciousness? For some reason I felt the need to defend Gertrude Stein. Every century needs an artist to dismantle coherence as we have been taught it and make a space for something new to happen.

8

Gertrude Stein was happier than Virginia Woolf, who understood how to make something coherently incoherent from human consciousness. Coherence was important to Woolf because she knew how it felt to mentally disintegrate, to believe birds were singing in ancient Greek. Yes, Woolf was the more skilled writer, the genius who worked hard for modernism through English rain, boiled cabbage and endless patriarchy. She was slightly bewildered by Walt Whitman's talent for joy when she wrote, 'He could sink into a reverie of bliss over the scent of an orange.' And then she walked into the River Ouse, aged fifty-nine, to drown herself.

Gertrude Stein began writing The Autobiography of Alice B. Toklas when she was fifty-eight, the book that gave her the gloire she craved. It was writing about herself in the voice of Alice B. Toklas that freed her own voice, revealed the cadence of her sentences and her fluent, slightly strange prose. Alice B. narrates the book. At first we believe that she is indeed writing her autobiography. After a few pages, it becomes clear as mud that Gertrude Stein is writing about herself through the lips of her lover and companion. This is the book from which Stein vulgarly earned some money that was not inherited wealth. Stein was unfashionably good at life and happy in love. All the same, Virginia Woolf, born six years after Gertrude Stein, is the writer I have found most encouraging in every phase in life.

She thought so deeply. For me.
And what about Gertrude Stein?
She thought deeply.

It is entirely necessary for a writer to dismantle realism as we have been taught it and put together a new composition. Gertrude Stein, whose apartment in Montparnasse did not have electricity until 1914, made a space for John Cage to happen. He wanted to dismantle the grammar of Western music because he was bored with 'its endless arrangements of old sounds'. In 1932, he set three short texts by Stein to music, intuiting that in some ways they were both walking in the same direction towards the future.

'The Stein songs are, so to speak, transcriptions from a repetitive language to a repetitive music,' he wrote.

Six years later he would meet the love of his life, the choreographer Merce Cunningham, who dismantled the language of ballet and made something new with it. No plot. No story.

Meanwhile, in the early twentieth century, Auguste Rodin is following Isadora Duncan around Europe, sketching thousands of drawings of her dancing for curious audiences, barefoot and uncorseted. Isadora Duncan, who broke away from the rigid grammar of ballet, made a space for Merce Cunningham to happen. All of this was part of the streams of consciousness flowing and overflowing through modernism. Reeds and mint, wild geranium, duckweed and lilies sometimes grew on the edge of the streams.

9

The electrique was placed in the centre of the table, a pot of boiled potatoes perched on top of it. Fanny had to order the Raclette in advance so it could be cut to fit into the little pans that slid under the grill. Her assistant had organized a plate of salami and a bowl of tiny gherkins to accompany the melting Alpine cheese. Her assistant was Eva the Fifth, of course. Fanny had some information for us. 'Raclette was invented by Swiss shepherds in the twelfth century.' Her phone bleeped. I knew she was going to be speaking to Lucia, who had more information about the cat that had drowned in the Canal Saint-Martin. Fanny was pretending to make a work call, but she found time to tell us (again) that Raclette is sweet and earthy and instructed us to place the little pans under the grill of the electrique.

'I don't like that word earthy, do you mean it tastes of soil?' Eva wanted to know.

'O-kaay, it's not earthy,' Fanny replied, phone pressed against her ear. She was standing behind Eva's chair, gazing at the books on her shelves. A small aerosol spray stood in-between two of the books. When I looked more closely I saw it was called WD-40. It promised, in capital letters, to quieten squeaking, loosen rusted parts and to free mechanisms that have become stuck. This seemed to me an excellent tutorial for writing my essay on Gertrude Stein. The melting Raclette was making me feel slightly sick.

Eva cut her potato in half. 'I think when Fanny says earthy, she means the Raclette tastes of the grass that grows in the pastures and valleys.'

'Yeah, that's right.' Fanny kissed Eva on the top of her head.

The Raclette was now sizzling in its pans while Fanny paced the room and spoke to

Lucia. We were not exactly shivering in a chalet in the snows of the Savoy. Fanny's apartment was warm, light, white, spacious and modern. We could wave to our reflection on the parquet floors and had been instructed, in a low voice by Fanny, to take off our shoes, as if she were suggesting something intimate to one of her three lovers.

'If there's a war we should all travel to the Swiss countryside and take a morphine tablet to end our lives in the Alpine meadows,' Eva whispered to me.

Fanny interrupted her call to instruct us to take the pan from under the grill and slide the melting Raclette over a potato. 'Please help yourself to the charcuterie and cornichons.'

'Yes,' she said to Lucia on the phone, 'I got it, thanks for your thoughts, buy and hold is the way to proceed.'

Fanny's apartment began to smell as if she kept a herd of cows in the hallway.

Eva and I scraped the cheese from our pans and tipped it on to a potato. It was hot, earthy and creamy. Now that Eva had got the subject of suicide amongst the goats and cows of Switzerland off her chest, she returned to the subject of Gertrude Stein.

'Fanny has earned her own money since she was sixteen. Unlike Gertrude Stein, who never had to take a job to pay her bills.' Her eyes were so blue, just looking at Eva made me go Awww. There was a lot of pain in her eyes. Maybe it was more like Owww. For some reason she was still whispering.

'I think the peaceful times are over. Poland now wants all adult men to train in the military. And the European countries are just biding their time.'

Fanny finished her call and placed her phone by the side of her plate.

'Eva will be Secretary of Defence in my new administration,' she said, her face neutral like Switzerland as she flipped the molten Raclette over a slice of salami.

After a while Eva interrupted the silence in the manner of Jane Austen.

'Does it always rain through November in Paris?'

'Well, I have some news,' Fanny finally announced. She was head of the table. After all, she was the only one of us who was not lonely and foreign.

'I am sorry to have to tell you that a cat with a white belly was found in the Saint-Martin canal.'

We waited while she pierced a small onion with the prong of her fork.

'Indeed, one ear was shorter than the other. In every way it resembles Bob.'

Eva had stopped eating and was touching the ends of her fringe.

'I instructed Lucia to look at the cat closely for me. I mean, is it o-kaay to ask my lover to look so closely at death? Believe me, Lucia would rather look at the mole on my left thigh.'

She shrugged and waved her fork in the air. And then she smiled.

'Time to crack open the eau de vie,' she said, gathering three small glasses and placing them on the table.

'The cat was ginger and Bob is not ginger.'

Eau de vie. The water of life. Fanny had

been treading the water of death while Eva had been climbing the alps of death. Did she not fully understand that Eva was in a desperate situation with her husband who lived in Seattle? They had unfashionably married when Eva was nineteen, pledging for ever and ever and ever and ever when they were art students together in Berlin. Eva was now thirty-three and had been married for fourteen years. I thought that Fanny was somewhat sadistic in the way she had delivered this information. Yet Eva seemed more interested in my essay on Gertrude Stein. She ignored Fanny and instructed me to focus again on William James. What did he see in Stein that other professors might have missed? It was William James who had suggested she study medicine. It was the route to her becoming a psychologist.

10

Gertrude Stein's interest in psychology was set ablaze by the sight of a man hitting a woman with an umbrella on one of her lonely walks after her mother died. At the time, her family lived in Oakland, California. She wanted to know why he behaved in that way.

At nineteen, Stein must have been more worldly than most of the female students at Radcliffe College for young women. She had travelled with her parents to Vienna and Paris as a child. On her third birthday, her long brown hair curled into ringlets around her shoulders, she was allowed to take one small sip of Austrian beer. The Stein children were taught by a Hungarian and a Czech tutor. English was not the only language they heard in their various homes. After a year in Paris when she was four, she returned to America with a microscope and a French history of zoology. These were the objects that would haunt the future, given she was going to train in the laboratories of Harvard and Johns Hopkins. After their parents died, the Stein siblings lived with their mother's family in Baltimore. Their aunt was shocked to discover they did not sleep in pyjamas. The college girls in the stuffy air of 1893 regarded Gertrude Stein as rather eccentric, ungainly, sweaty, maybe too Jewish, too something other. She thought they were dull, physically weak, conformist, neurotic and illogical. She did not want to become a woman in this mode. Yet at the same time she was sexually attracted to women. How would she define her difference from them if these illogical young women both seduced and wounded her? Stein became secretary of the philosophy debating club, made good friends, wore a jaunty sailor's cap, smoked cigars, rode her bicycle and went on long hikes. It was agreed amongst the female students that should a male predator walk too near them on one of these hikes, plump Gertrude Stein would climb up a tree and fall on him.

It was becoming tragically obvious to Stein, as she sat in the laboratory dissecting various specimens preserved in alcohol, that she must never sit at the far end of the table making conversation with the wife of a male genius. She would need to become the genius herself. Her future wife, Alice B., would be delegated to make conversation with the wives of famous men while Gertrude made big talk with the men who visited her collection of outlaw art.

Frankly, with a few exceptions, I would have preferred to talk to the wives. I don't believe there's such a thing as small talk. It's likely the wives would ask me a few questions about my own life and I am entirely interested in their lives. Particularly in Madame Cézanne, Hortense Fiquet, wife of Paul Cézanne, who read her insomniac husband the poetry of Baudelaire for hours at night to help him sleep. After a while, they lived separately for much of their marriage. Monsieur Cézanne apparently complained that his wife was only interested in lemonade and Switzerland.

Madame Cézanne, please can we discuss Switzerland?

I understand you met your husband when you were nineteen at the Swiss Academy, where you worked as a bookbinder and part-time artist's model to earn some extra money. You sat for twenty-seven iconic portraits painted by your husband and were criticized for having a somewhat unsmiling, impenetrable expression in the portraits. Is it true he kept your long relationship hidden from his own parents for many years (including the birth of your child) for fear his family would sever his allowance?

Madame Cézanne leans forwards and smacks my knuckles with her fan. 'Please,' she says, 'I wish to talk only of lemonade.'

Gertrude Stein was later to be inspired by Cézanne's portrait of intense, unhappy Hortense Fiquet, seated on a red chair holding a fan. She bought it with her brother Leo and couldn't stop looking at it. It was Cézanne, she said, who taught her about composition, but her first major influence was William James. He was the professor who had admired her, been entertained by her, when she was at Radcliffe. His lectures blew her mind and it's possible she never recovered. William James, who was instrumental in establishing Harvard's first psychology department, was startled by this eccentric, chaotic young woman sitting in his lectures, hair dishevelled, awarding her top marks when she wrote him a note to explain she would prefer to go to the opera than sit an exam. 'I have often felt the same way, myself,' he replied. William James, author of the groundbreaking Principles of Psychology (1890), widely read in North America and Europe, including by Jung and Freud, regarded Gertrude Stein as his most brilliant student. Why? Perhaps it was something to do with how, in her own words, she was 'tremendously occupied with finding out what was inside myself to make what I was'.

*

Brother of the novelist Henry James, William James was humorous, lively and fragile. He had suffered from depression, anguish, suicidal thoughts in his own younger years. He had to argue with himself about why life is worth living. When he taught his students he would sometimes stretch out on the floor in his brown tweed suit to write on his handheld blackboard. The most useful consciousness, he insisted in Principles of Psychology, is 'found in personal consciousness, minds, selves, concrete particular I's and you's'.

Including the wives, I presume.

Jack Kerouac was influenced by William James too. Kerouac called his own writing 'spontaneous prose'.

'. . . the only people for me are the mad ones, the ones who are mad to live, mad to talk, mad to be saved, desirous of everything at the same time, the ones who never yawn or say a commonplace thing, but burn, burn, burn like fabulous yellow roman candles exploding like spiders across the stars and in the middle you see the blue center-light pop and everybody goes "Awww!"'

On the Road (1957)

What else was it in William James that responded to nineteen-year-old Gertrude Stein? Why would he award her top marks for not attending an exam? It was he who had suggested she go on to study medicine at Johns Hopkins. It was the route, he suggested, to pursue her interest in women's nervous disorders.

Perhaps he had seen through some of Stein's youthful bravado.

She was an orphan by the time she arrived at Harvard Annex in 1893, the college for women that was to become Radcliffe College. Her mother had died when she was fourteen and her father died three years later. It is not surprising she was going to make 'existence' and 'presence' her subject.

The sister of William James, Alice James, most famous for the diary she kept in her last few years, did not want to exist or be present at all. Alice was even more anguished than her brother. She had suffered extreme breakdowns and had taken to her bed. Susan Sontag wrote a play about her, titled Alice in Bed. Alice had spoken to her father about the ethics of taking her own life. He agreed that suffering that was unbearable was not a way to live. Yes, he said, she could take her life, if she did it gently. Her father's transgressive permission somehow gave Alice James an appetite for life. She was also in love with a teacher and early advocate of education for women, Katharine Peabody Loring, who nursed and loved her to the end. They were intellectual companions and romantic companions. Alice James wrote about Katharine in a letter to Sarah Sedgwick Darwin in 1879:

'I wish you could know Katharine Loring. She is a most wonderful being. She had all the mere brute superiority which distinguishes man from woman combined with all the distinctly feminine virtues. There is nothing she cannot do from hewing wood and drawing water to driving run-away horses and educating all the women in North America.'

Katharine had become part of the James family. Perhaps William, who was close to his sister, might have understood Gertrude Stein in ways that no one else in her new community of scholars and students was equipped to do. Stein also wanted brute superiority. It was a better option than the other options available to women of her generation: marriage, taking to her bed, everyday brute inferiority. Men did the thinking. Women did the feeling. What was she to do with her own feelings if she wanted brute superiority? In the meanwhile, she co-wrote a paper on the subject of female hysteria, exploring the phenomenon of women who had 'a double personality'.

All of this was part of the streams of consciousness, described by William James as the 'movement of thoughts and words endlessly the same and endlessly different'. Gertrude Stein would forever write sentences that were endlessly the same and endlessly different.

*

I had dived into the streams and was clinging to the sides.

James had invited Stein to set up a clinical automatic writing experiment in the laboratory at Harvard, decades before the surrealist art movement became interested in similar strategies to explore the unconscious mind. André Breton, the chief theoretical spokesperson for the surrealist movement in Europe, regarded automatic writing as a 'true photography of thought', yet Stein, two decades earlier, regarded automatic writing as an *excess of consciousness.*

On and on the streams of consciousness in all their excess overflowed while the November elections in America raged on. And somewhere in a field alongside the streams in the nineteenth century was Walt Whitman, broad shoulders, open shirt, the father of free verse, strangely modern in 1855, sucking a blade of grass under the big American sky.

'This is what you shall do: Love the earth and sun and the animals, despise riches, give

alms to every one that asks, stand up for the stupid and crazy, devote your income and labor to others, hate tyrants, argue not concerning God . . .'
    Leaves of Grass

Was this the only way to live or an impossible way to live or just how Walt Whitman lived?

'To Whitman there was nothing unbefitting the dignity of a human being in the acceptance either of money or of underwear.'
    Virginia Woolf, 'Visits to Walt Whitman', Times Literary Supplement (1918)

America's roaming poet laureate made sure he signed a copy of Leaves of Grass for Peter Doyle, a streetcar conductor, his most cherished lover. Perhaps Eva's cat was swimming through one of the streams of consciousness near Walt Whitman as he lay in a field dreaming of Peter. Yes, Bob was floating in the streams, his golden eyes wide open, onwards through the nineteenth century, past the perfumed flowers of Charles Baudelaire's 'strangeness is a necessary ingredient in beauty', past the avant-garde movements and moments of the twentieth century, arriving shattered and dripping in the evening twilight of our own century.

11

The twenty-first century was in its twenties. Always a turbulent time. We were the lucky ones. We were not under the rubble. We were on our screens, scrolling, scrolling, scrolling through the various wars in the twenty-fourth year of the twenty-first century. In-between writing my essay on Gertrude Stein and scrolling through the news I walked out to the market to buy sweet, crisp apples from Normandy. Sometimes I thought about Gertrude Stein when she was approaching her sixtieth year. Sitting in the garden of her country home with her little dog resting behind her neck. Alice B. would wake at six in the morning to pick strawberries for her breakfast. It was hard to get a sense of Gertrude Stein's age because her writing was so adventurous.

12

'Oh, we're all screwed,' Fanny said when the result from the American elections hit our screens in Paris.

'I'm off to scream into the Seine.'

Fanny had Lucia to distract her, Eva was engrossed in the drawings for her graphic novel and I was alone being numbed up by Gertrude Stein.

> 'Lovely snipe and tender turn, excellent vapor and slender butter,
> all the splinter and the trunk, all the poisonous darkening drunk,
> all the joy in weak success, all the joyful tenderness,

all the section and the tea, all the stouter symmetry.'
Tender Buttons

What was it that Fanny had told us about the small black mole on the inside of her left thigh?

She told us she had always considered it to be an imperfection. Yet Lucia liked to kiss it, which, Fanny informed us, was like 'being touched by a fern in twilight'. This is how Fanny spoke about Lucia. Our job was to listen and nod as if we were her students taking notes at the Sorbonne. Fanny was the only one of us who claimed to have had a happy childhood. She often told me how she liked to return to her village, a one-hour drive from Avignon, to play boules with her father and his friends. It was a good way to catch up on local gossip. They were legendary players, she said, and her mother was a nurse, retired now, but I would admire her because she swam every day in the river. Her mother liked rain because it boded well for deeper swimming in the summer months.

*

It felt like winter had arrived in Paris. I met Eva for a walk. I thought she might want to talk about Hamish in Seattle on this day of all days, his plans, her plans, what he thought about it all. By 'it all' did I mean fascism or authoritarianism or something near it?

No one could bring themselves to dig up the grimy old fascism word from the twentieth century and paste it on to the twenty-first century, or to say things like 'never again' or to exclaim, in regard to officials and armies who participate in ethnic cleansing, 'I just don't understand how humans can obey those sorts of orders.' No one wanted to dig it all up, to dig up the twentieth century and find Hannah Arendt in 1947, dust on the shoulders of her suit jacket, a pack of cigarettes in her pocket, speaking calmly to them on the banality of evil in their own century. To us. In our own century. All of this was part of the streams of consciousness flowing under the mowed and manicured golf courses on which men swung their clubs in the twenty-first century. Gertrude Stein had lived through some of it.

*

What is it?

Colonialism. Fascism. Communism. Alienation. Disorientation. Fragmentation. Dislocation. Fauvism. Impressionism. Cubism. Futurism. Dadaism. Surrealism. Modernism.

The art that Stein collected was made with some of these isms and ions.

Instead of digging up Hamish in Seattle, Eva told me that Fanny had bought a bulldog for Lucia. A pug. Apparently, it didn't like moonlight and preferred walking at night under a cloudy sky. Also, the pug would only sleep next to Lucia's childhood rocking horse and refused to drink water. Fanny was wondering if the pug was a hysteric who in 1880 would have been handed over to the neurologist known as the Napoleon of Neuroses, Professor Charcot, at the Salpêtrière Hospital.

'We didn't tell you because we know you are busy with your essay on Gertrude Stein and have more important things to think about.'

Eva, who was oversensitive, knew that I felt

excluded from this news. Was the new pug less important than my essay on Gertrude Stein? Perhaps this was a question for Bob, who had been drifting through the streams. Why a bulldog? Apparently, the French breed liked living in apartments and did not need too much exercise. It was playful, affectionate, and Lucia suffered from obsessive thoughts when she was alone in the dark at night. If her thoughts kept her awake (the Seine flooding, a new pain below her ribs, unstable powerful men, forest fires, her bank card being declined in a supermarket, phoning her ageing father's carer and no one picking up, the way her boss poked her fingers deep into her own eye when she was angry — maybe it was some kind of masochism that made her boss need to hurt herself — always the left eye, which made Lucia worry the world was full of people desiring punishment who secretly wanted the world to end before she had even finished writing the conclusion to her PhD, which might help her get a job she actually enjoyed rather than endured, though since meeting Fanny she was suffering from vertigo and confusion and losing the thread to her thesis and no longer believed she was contributing new knowledge to her field, which meant she had to rewrite the conclusion and dig the field for newness while she struggled to pay her bills), when all this made her panic, she could read her 'How to Live with a Dog' manual. Did it give advice on what to do about the pug refusing to drink water? Yes, it did. Eva told me they filled the pug's bowl with coconut water in the day and in the evenings fed it with chicken broth. Meanwhile, we couldn't resist scrolling through the news on our phones to see what was happening in America, where Gertrude Stein was born. Eva's fingers also lingered on some drawings she had made that afternoon and loaded on to her phone. Her graphic novel had now swerved to the subject of how to live without a cat. There was nothing about how to live without a husband. I had thought she kept fruit ripening on her window ledge to have something to look forward to in the future, but glancing at her phone, I saw she had painted the persimmon. It did look quite suicidal perched precariously on the ledge. She had composed an aeriel view of the fruit and the five floors beneath it. Was the persimmon a surrogate for her cat, or had she projected aspects of herself into the persimmon, or was it just a still life?

The sun was setting as we stood on the Pont Saint-Louis. A tourist boat lit with tiny golden bulbs wreathed around the rails moved slowly through the waters of the Seine. Someone was playing a trumpet under the bridge. The boat would stop at Notre-Dame, Hôtel de Ville, Louvre, Saint-Germain-des-Prés, Musée d'Orsay, Place de la Concorde, Invalides, Eiffel Tower. Perhaps a few of the tourists disembarking at Saint-Germain-des-Prés would look for the ghosts of Juliette Gréco and Serge Gainsbourg, who had once lived near there. What did they know about these two glamorous singer-poets? What did I know?

In 1943, Juliette Gréco's mother (who had joined the Resistance) and Juliette's sister, Charlotte, were arrested by the Gestapo and deported to the concentration camp in Ravensbrück. They managed to survive until liberation in 1945. Juliette Gréco was haunted by her own arrest and release by the Gestapo (she was sixteen) and by her sister and mother's suffering for the rest of her life. Jean-Paul Sartre wrote her a few songs. He reckoned Gréco had 'a million poems in her voice'. As a teenager Serge Gainsbourg was forced to wear the yellow star the Nazis and the French Vichy government imposed on Jews. Who in his family would have sewed it on his jacket? Or did he sew it himself? Where is the needle, where is the thread?

That's the good thing about being a tourist. We can pass through history on a boat lit up with little golden bulbs.

I sometimes liked to play 'Je T'Aime . . . Moi Non Plus' when Gertrude Stein was getting on my nerves. In fact, I told Eva that Serge Gainsbourg's two sentences together, 'I love you . . . me neither', were better than anything Gertrude Stein had ever written.

'You've finally shocked me,' Eva said, waving back to the tourists on the boat. We both laughed and soon all the tourists were waving at us. 'Je T'Aime . . . Moi Non Plus' had probably been banned in all their countries, including America, where it had climbed up the charts but got stuck on number 69.

There were many Americans living in Paris. Some of them were our friends. After the election they were mostly talking about Switzerland and lemonade. Gertrude Stein was a republican and a libertarian, what would she have made of it all?

'After all everybody, that is, everybody who writes is interested in living inside themselves in order to tell what is inside themselves.

That is why writers have to have two countries, the one where they belong and the one in which they live really.'

Paris France (1940) by Gertrude Stein

Eva suddenly whipped off my fur hat and pretended to throw it to the tourists waving from the boat on the Seine. 'I believe Gertrude would have passed her medical exams if she hadn't inherited money from her family.' If the tourists on the boat could have seen Eva's blue eyes, they would have all gone Awww.

13

In 1903 Gertrude Stein began her new life in Europe with a full medical training yet without her degree. She had failed four of her nine final-year exams at Johns Hopkins when she arrived in Paris to join her brother. In photographs she looks glum, tired, more defeated at twenty-nine than she will ever look afterwards. She apparently gave advice to friends about pneumonia and how to feed babies. She was very nearly a doctor. Her mind was possibly full of the neurology of the embryo while she walked through the Luxembourg Gardens and noticed the pigeons strutting around the grass on which no human was allowed to walk or sit or laze. When she wrote the libretto for an opera that transferred to Broadway in America, it was haunted by pigeons in Paris. Virgil Thompson was its innovative composer, who, when he studied at Harvard, had been enchanted by the piano compositions of Eric Satie.

'Pigeons on the grass alas.

Pigeons on the grass alas.

Short longer grass short longer longer shorter yellow grass. Pigeons large pigeons on the shorter longer yellow grass alas pigeons on the grass.'

Four Saints in Three Acts (1927)

Stein moved in with her older brother Leo, who was living in a rented apartment in Montparnasse, 27 Rue de Fleurus. Why had his youngest, most brilliant sister failed four out of nine final exams? Her story was that she was irrevocably bored by her studies. It must have been a relief to take off the tight clothes she wore as a medical student and dress like a monk in loose-fitting brown robes and open Greek sandals. Isadora Duncan's brother had designed the sandals.

I can hear her thinking about how to put herself together. She was massive when women were supposed to be miniature, an intellectual when women were supposed to be domesticated, queer when she was supposed to be straight. Maybe she looked more like a cardinal than a monk. Thankfully her corset was now floating down one of the streams of consciousness. Perhaps a nineteenth-century swan had built a nest with it. The great couturier Pierre Balmain would come to the rescue and make her some suits and coats and a brown velvet cap.

Sometimes I think about her walking through Paris in her open sandals, three years after Oscar Wilde's lonely death in what was then the Hôtel d'Alsace, on the Left Bank. Stein had discovered her own unreciprocated sexual desires for a female student when she was at medical school. To have been in love and then rejected had taken 'all the sunshine' out of her day. She must have known about the brutal way Wilde had been punished for his homosexuality. In England, E. M. Forster was aware of the crushing of Wilde, his senseless, shocking, solitary death in exile. Leo would have offered his unmarried sister some societal protection from that kind of atmosphere. Their sister-in-law Sarah Stein had sent Gertrude a letter when she was still a student insisting that the route to supreme happiness was marriage and birthing babies.

Leo might have been moody, clever, neurotic and hypercritical, but he was very beloved to Gertrude. She had always been the one closest to him in the family. They were intellectually entranced by each other. He was as thin as she was large and suffered from gastric problems. If Leo was always fasting, Gertrude was always feasting. Perhaps he should have been handed over to Professor Charcot along with Fanny and Lucia's moon-phobic pug. He had never completed any of his studies. Two years older than Gertrude, he had attended college at Berkeley, Johns Hopkins and Harvard, which he left in 1895 to sail around the world. Isn't that what rich men do? Having flirted with biology, philosophy, literature, psychology and art history, he now wanted to be an artist. He was attempting to write and was interested in various theories of visual perception, yet would publish his A-B-C of Aesthetics decades later. To his horror, it was his baby sister who was up all night writing at her desk. There she is. Pen. Ink. The light of a gas lamp. She is writing all the time. It did not occur to Leo Stein to paint his sister's portrait.

That would be left to Picasso.

When they began to buy art together, he knew much more about it than she did. First it was the work of Toulouse-Lautrec, Gauguin, Renoir, Degas, and then they started to buy modern 'outlaw' art when it was cheap. Cézanne, Matisse, Picasso, Braque, Gris.

Leo and Gertrude were startled by the radical vision of these artists at a time when they were unknown and could be bought cheaply. The paintings that were going to become priceless were hung in their apartment on every inch of the walls, from floor to ceiling. On Saturday evenings, Leo and Gertrude opened their door to writers, dancers, avant-garde poets and artists who were curious to see this disorientating new art and to listen to Leo talk about it. At that time they did not have electricity at 27 Rue de Fleurus. How did they light the art that lit up the twentieth century? With gas lamps. An oil lamp. By striking a match. To have been young and alive when this new visual language emerged (Cézanne, Matisse, Picasso) might have blown away Gertrude's sense of failure at not resitting her medical exams. She listened attentively to Leo and she was writing all the time, lit up by the belief that she was on to something big and new. She was learning from Paul Cézanne and then from cubism (Picasso and Braque) that composition *is* the explanation, which most writers know anyway. Stein came to literature from a medical training and knew more about tuberculosis than the slog of composition.

Gertrude Stein and Picasso met when she was thirty-one and he was twenty-four. She describes the first time he came to dinner with her and Leo in The Autobiography of Alice B. Toklas, the book that lit up her name in Times Square, New York, with the words GERTRUDE STEIN HAS ARRIVED.

Stein and Toklas would meet Charlie Chaplin and Josephine Baker and somehow not manage to fit F. Scott Fitzgerald into their schedule.

But first Picasso had to arrive.

'He was thin dark, alive with big pools of eyes and a violent but not rough way. He was sitting next to Gertrude Stein at dinner and she took up a piece of bread. This, said Picasso, snatching it back with violence, this piece of bread is mine. She laughed and he looked sheepish. That was the beginning of their intimacy.'
    The Autobiography of Alice B. Toklas

Gertrude Stein was the genius in residence and not the angel of the house. Picasso had painted her portrait in 1906, mostly because he was jealous of Matisse's portrait of his wife, Amélie Matisse, Femme au Chapeau. In the winter afternoons, Gertrude Stein would take the horse-pulled omnibus across Paris and up the hill to his studio in Montmartre, an old piano factory with one toilet between many artists.

Did Gertrude have to pull up her monkish robes and squat over a hole? She did not have a bourgeois sensibility though she led a comfortable life. When she learned to drive she would have one hand on the steering wheel and a roast chicken leg in the other. Stein posed for Picasso about eighty times. On her long walk home to Rue de Fleurus in her Greek sandals, was she pleased she had not become a medical doctor?

She was becoming something.
    She was going to write about Picasso.
    She was inventing a language.
    She would make up some rules about grammar.
    No question marks. No commas.
    She had no idea what she was doing. She was just doing it. All art has to start like that.

While Gertrude sat for Picasso she was thinking about the novellas she was writing at the time, Three Lives. And she was also writing a novel, The Making of Americans, apparently about a fictional middle-class American family who resembled her own middle-class immigrant family. On and on she wrote until she eventually finished it in 1911. She wanted to tell the story of 'a family's progress', how anger fear anxiety aggression are passed on through generations of a family and then repeated in every human that has ever lived. If it was an audacious idea, Sigmund Freud had the same idea too. Stein pulls herself, the author, into the book as a writing presence, telling readers she is scribbling on scraps of lined paper in this endless investigation of what she called 'bottom character'.

Writing was Stein's way of avoiding everything. It seems to me that repetition was her way of moving closer to her enquiry but never getting there. After all, what might she find? Find *there*. I'm not sure 'bottom character' interested her as much as she thought it did. Is it exciting to put things in the way of being understood? I think it is. I often do that myself. Put things in the way. Yet, to be relentlessly transparent or relentlessly opaque is not how the human mind is wired. Gertrude Stein, the daughter of immigrants, was convinced she had arrived on undiscovered literary land. When she later wrote about Picasso, she returned to many of her own thoughts in The Making of Americans.

'People really do not change from one generation to another, as far back as we know history people are about the same as they were, they have the same needs, the same desires, the same virtues and the same qualities, the same defects, indeed nothing changes from one generation to another except the things seen and the things seen make that generation . . .'
 Picasso (1938) by Gertrude Stein

While Picasso was painting her portrait, he couldn't paint her head. Perhaps she was transmitting Stein-shaped sentences to his paintbrush. A Stein-shaped sentence is a very bespoke thing. No wonder he had to flee to Spain to recover. When he returned to Paris, he did not summon her to sit for him and instead finished the head in her absence. It resembled a mask with long lidded eyes. He had reached for her 'bottom character' and discovered it was masked. I suspect he could not paint the face of a woman who did not sexually desire him or submit to his sadism in any other way. Stein is in command, her posture, her hands, her gaze, she is a thinking female subject in that portrait. Not a machine for suffering. Not a goddess, nor a doormat. If this was how Picasso viewed women, Stein was more like a machine for eating honeydew melons and jugged hare with redcurrants.

'I was and still am satisfied with my portrait, for me, it is I, and it is the only reproduction of me which is always I, for me.'
    Picasso by Gertrude Stein

Eleven years is a long time to live with a sibling. To live with any member of a family. E. M. Forster, who lived for much of his life with his mother in a genteel village in Surrey, described how he would 'climb to the top of the downs, and look longingly towards industrialism and London'.
    Industrialism is also floating in the streams

of consciousness that will empty into modernism and modernisms.

I had to remind myself that to collect art you have to see something new that has not been seen before. Above all, you must know how to defend it, how to talk about it, and, as Stein insisted, you have to love something that your own generation might find ugly. At first she had no idea how to talk about it. What was it? The art. Her training in early psychology with William James had given her some tools to perceive and grasp this emerging language, but she did not know how to apply it to her own writing. She was working it out. Perhaps she never worked it out. She had travelled a long way from the nineteenth century. To travel a long way from the realism of any century is a perilous journey. The streets will be lined with people mocking the new and the strange – educated, uneducated, it doesn't matter, they will be righteous and wrathful in the cause of realism in every century.

*

Stein listened to her brother until she knew how to work with this new visual language, had moved closer to it through her own writing, closer to its purpose and importance. It was not just about owning art and displaying it, but owning its radical way of seeing. Owning what Virginia Woolf described as a change in the way human character was perceived. Its composition. How it was put together. Or, in Stein's words, 'how things were seen'.

When Leo and Gertrude hosted their salon at 27 Rue de Fleurus in Montparnasse, it might have been a good idea to invite Matisse to talk about Cézanne, instead of Leo. When he was struggling and hungry, Matisse had bought Cézanne's painting Three Bathers, the composition that gave Matisse courage for thirty-seven years. He paid for that painting in instalments so he could feed his family and heat his studio.

In 1910 the English art critic Roger Fry curated a controversial exhibition in the Grafton Galleries in London, which he titled 'Manet and the Post-Impressionists'. It included the work of Cézanne, Gauguin, Manet, Matisse, Picasso and Van Gogh. Some of the British public were outraged, lamenting the show was 'the outpouring of the lunatic asylum'.

Yet the Steins had got there first. Gertrude and Leo had bought Matisse's Femme au Chapeau after it scandalized the Salon d'Automne in 1905. People had tried to scratch the paint off the canvas with their thumbs. Someone had written on the front door of this exhibition, 'Gallery of dangerous lunatics – enter at your own risk'. Perhaps this person was so sane he was just a little bit mad.

When the American photographer Alfred Stieglitz came to see the pictures hung in the atelier at 27 Rue de Fleurus with Edward Steichen, he describes how Stein, a woman whose name he did not hear, reclined in the dark on a chaise longue and did not speak a word while her brother spoke 'beautiful English' for ninety minutes.

*

' "I found myself in a huge room. Paintings covered the walls from floor nearly to ceiling . . . Books and papers covered a long table, very long, at which sat a bald man with eyeglasses and whiskers. Elsewhere in the room I noticed a woman, dark and bulksome.

Steichen introduced me to the man, Leo Stein, and to the woman, whose name I did not hear. No one else was present." '

Alfred Stieglitz: Introduction to an American Seer (1960) by Dorothy Norman

Leo, Edward, Alfred.

Alfred Stieglitz only realized the nameless woman sitting in the shadows was Gertrude Stein after he published her word portraits, or what she called word paintings, of Picasso and Matisse in his magazine, Camera Work, in 1912.

Gertrude Stein was becoming something.
    She was losing it.
    She had to.
    What was it?
    Being nameless. Sitting in the shadows.

No one had asked her what she was writing or even knew she was writing, or what she was thinking, or even cared about what she was thinking. She was Leo's silent sister.

Thirty years later, on her 1934 American book tour for The Autobiography of Alice B. Toklas, when her publisher, Bennett Cerf at American Random House, hosted a live radio show with her, he kicked off by saying, 'I'm very proud to be your publisher, Miss Stein, but as I've always told you, I don't understand very much of what you're saying.' Gertrude replied, 'Well, I've always told you Bennett, you're a very nice boy but you're rather stupid.' This was bravado considering she needed him more than he needed her. Bennett took it in his stride: 'Believe me, I didn't kid around with Gertrude for the rest of the interview. I was very respectful. She was superb, especially when she started explaining herself' (At Random: The Reminiscences of Bennett Cerf (1977)).

Gertrude had lost it.

What is it?
Being undermined.
The temptation to smile it off.

I don't understand her either.

I can't wait to return to Fanny's pug and Eva's melancholy eyes, Owww, and the apples from Normandy in the Tuesday market.

Stein stood her ground with Ezra Pound too. When he called her 'that tub of guts', she called him 'A village explainer, excellent if you were a village, but if you were not, not.' Perhaps he reminded her of Leo. Stein was hurt that Pound had not published her writing when he was so devoted to the modernists of his era: James Joyce, William Butler Yeats, Robert Frost, William Carlos Williams, Ernest Hemingway, Ford Madox Ford and Marianne Moore.

Perhaps the only thing Pound and Stein had in common was that he supported Mussolini, and she was a republican libertarian who was going to translate some of Pétain's speeches into English during World War II. No one knows if she was trying to save her life in 1941 or if she believed in the values of Pétain. It's as clear as mud. When Freud was forced to leave Vienna in 1938 he was required to sign a document to confirm he was not mistreated by the Nazis in any way. He unscrewed the top from his fountain pen and wrote, 'I can most highly recommend the Gestapo to everyone.'

Somehow this is clear.

All of this was part of the overflowing streams of consciousness and they would all intermingle and flow and empty into modernism and modernisms and no one knows where it begins and ends.

14

Fanny thinks we should persuade Eva to go on a night search for it who was now Bob. We could make an agreeable night out of a sad situation, take torches, beers, stroll a few streets in the neighbourhood. We would walk gently into the autumn night and maybe without the noise of day we might enter Bob's secret hiding place. She also said that now Bob had gone missing, Eva and her husband had stopped talking on FaceTime. Another thing, Fanny said, one of us will have to carry one of those contraptions you put an animal inside to take it to the vet. Eva looked horrified when we told her about our idea. 'I have never put it in a cage. I will hold it in my arms under my coat and keep it calm.' Awww. But love in the form of Bob who used to be it had already escaped her. And who knew about Hamish? Did she want to hold him in her arms and keep him calm? And what about Eva? Who was holding her in their arms and keeping her calm? Actually, Eva did own one of those contraptions, we had seen it in the cupboard under the kitchen sink. Two days ago, at the Marché des Enfants Rouges in the Marais, the oldest covered food market in Paris, a grey striped kitten had skipped under the tables of the Moroccan place that Eva and I had chosen to have lunch. Eva scooped it up and fed it slivers of chicken. The market was named after the children who wore red clothes at the orphanage next door, founded in the sixteenth century. Red was the colour that symbolized Christian charity and it was also the colour of Eva's lipstick. She told me that her graphic novel was about her family, which is why she was interested in The Making of Americans by Gertrude Stein. For this reason, Eva always carried it with her on her Kindle, so we read a few pages together while the kitten slept on her knee.

*

'There was a man who was always writing to his daughter that she should not do things that were wrong that would disgrace him, she should not do such things and in every letter that he wrote to her he told her she should not do such things, that he was her father and was giving good moral advice to her and always he wrote to her in every letter that she should not do things that she should not do anything that would disgrace him. He wrote this in every letter he wrote to her, he wrote very nicely to her, he wrote often enough to her and in every letter he wrote to her that she should not do anything that was a disgraceful thing for her to be doing and then once she wrote back to him that he had not any right to write moral things in letters to her, that he had taught her that he had shown her that he had commenced in her the doing the things things that would disgrace her and he had said then when he had begun with her he had said he did it so that when she was older she could take care of herself with those who wished to make her do things that were wicked things and he would teach her and she would be stronger than such girls who had not any way of knowing better, and she wrote this letter and her father got the letter and he was a paralytic always after, it was a shock to him getting such a letter, he kept saying over and over again that his daughter was trying to kill him and now she had done it and at the time he got the letter he was sitting by the fire and he threw the letter in the fire and his wife asked him what was the matter and he said it is Edith she is killing me, what, is she disgracing us said the mother, no said the father, she is killing me and that was all he said then of the matter and he never wrote another letter.'

The Making of Americans (1925) by Gertrude Stein

'I don't know what to make of this,' Eva said. 'Shall we talk about Switzerland and lemonade?'

'Anyway,' I replied, 'she found fathers "depressing", by which I think she generally meant patriarchy and then more particularly her own tyrannical volatile father, who was very depressing.'

It was a cold afternoon. Eva took off her cardigan and placed it over the kitten.

'Also,' I ventured, as if I were adding a condiment to a light-hearted conversation, 'Stein risks coherence on these pages. Sometimes I think her more baffling writing is the language she found for pain.'

'I personally think you have lost it,' Eva interrupted. 'It's obvious that The Making of Americans: Being a History of a Family's Progress is her greatest work, the first epic stretch of modernism written by a female writer. But I can see it's stressful for you so you're just focusing on Tender Buttons.'

Sometimes I think Eva is more into Gertrude Stein than I am.

Someone was shouting at us. It was the owner of the couscous place. He started to make his way at a brisk pace towards our table. Eva joked that his little striped kitten was no longer with us, but then he yanked up the cardigan under which it was sleeping and scooped it off her knee.

*

The only thing that interests Fanny about Gertrude Stein is that Stein's father made his fortune by investing in San Francisco cable cars. 'You are wasting your life writing about her,' she said to me. 'Do you want a few days in the south of France?'

15

We took the train from Gare de Lyon to Avignon. Fanny hired a car and we stayed in a grand stone villa at the top of a valley, an hour's drive from the station. Smoke plumed out of every chimney. It was cold and everyone had a fire going. The house belonged to one of Fanny's clients. He mostly lived in America and only stayed here with his family for the month of August. There were many oak trees in the surrounding woods which meant this was a place where truffles prospered, in this region, where the soil was limestone. Digging for black diamonds, which was what truffles were called, was something that appealed to Fanny, but the neighbour had already left two truffles for us on the table, along with a perfectly ripe Brillat-Savarin, a cheese mostly made from cream.

We had not thought about bringing provisions for this trip. Fanny sliced the Brillat-Savarin in two and placed slivers of the truffle between the slices. This was our lunch, which we ate on the terrace, shivering in our coats. Thankfully I was wearing my fur hat.

'If you come again in the summer, the jasmine climbs the walls, the lavender will hypnotize our eyes and we can swim in my mother's river.' Fanny told me her parents lived about five miles from this valley, but she had decided not to visit them. When I spoke to Eva about this on my phone (hiding in one of the three bathrooms) she said, 'Yes, Fanny's told you this bullshit story about playing pétanque with her father. In fact they don't get on at all and he kicked Fanny out of the family home when she was sixteen.'

Eva knows much more about Fanny than I do because they speak in French with each other. My lack of language has shut me out. The door is not exactly closed, it is ajar, perhaps latched on to a chain like Eva's door when her cat lived with her. Really, I know a few basic things about my new friends. Fanny has just turned forty, she lives alone, has many lovers and co-owns a pug. Eva likes to walk the city of Paris in the day and prefers to paint at night. And what about the pug. Does it have a name yet?

Someone had placed a Chinese lantern in a pear tree.

Fanny wore a white silk scarf over her head and sunglasses (no sun in evidence) while she plunged her acrylic jewelled nails into her client's tomato plants, 'to space them', while listening to Stromae's 'Formidable', currently our favourite song. Its lament that yesterday was a better day than today might even have reached the truffles hiding in their secret places near the oak trees.

The main cupboard in the kitchen was stocked with twelve boxes of American crackers, five bottles of pancake syrup and three more of a hot sauce from Nashville. Perhaps Fanny's client and his family felt homesick away from America for a month. When Alice B. arrived in France, she cooked for Gertrude 'the simple dishes I had eaten in the homes of the San Joaquin Valley in California—fricasseed chicken, corn bread, apple and lemon pie'. It is likely they were homesick too. I'm not sure she included the recipes for these dishes in The Alice B. Toklas Cook Book, but she relished the splendour of Omelette Aurore, sent to Victor Hugo by the writer and aristocrat George Sand. This involved eight eggs, heavy cream, candied fruit, marrons glacés, cherries, frangipani cream and mountains of melted butter.

Alice B. had lost it.
What is it?
Drudgery.
Housekeeping for her father, grandfather and brother.

When her mother died, she was twenty and unmarried. There was now a vacancy for a life of servitude in the family home. Alice B. was required to step into it, manage their servants and raise her ten-year-old brother. She was a cultured, daring young woman, but she was unmarried. As it turns out, that was the best thing she had going for her. When Alice B. moved in with Gertrude Stein, she was not the angel of the house, more the angel at the gate, the gatekeeper, certainly not the sort of angel her father had in mind. She was not Woolf's self-sacrificing angel either, she was the beloved and controlling partner at the centre of one of the most exciting avant-garde salons of the era. I am not sure the wives of male writers fared so well as Alice B.

Zelda Fitzgerald and Vivien Eliot both died in mental asylums.

Later that evening the sky was clear and bright. The pear tree with its Chinese lantern hanging on a branch swayed gently under all the galaxies, though only the Milky Way was visible to our eyes. Somewhere nearby, geese were honking at a tractor making its way across a field. I wondered if Fanny had brought me to this house to be closer to her family home, which somehow haunted this much grander house in the valley. I asked her this question in French.

'Maybe. I try not to feel it too much. O-kaay, I feel it all the time. Any one of the bathrooms in this house is bigger than the bedroom of my parents,' and then she told me that the hardest part of being thrown out of her family home for kissing a girl was leaving behind her childhood pug. For some reason this made me laugh. She laughed with me and even forgot to mock my fur hat. We ate the crackers, dipping them in the hot sauce from Nashville while she gazed at the Chinese lantern perched in the pear tree.

16

When I stand on Boulevard Raspail near Auguste Rodin's statue of Balzac, I see the spectre of Gertrude Stein standing there with Pablo Picasso in 1914. It is night. Stein is forty. Picasso is thirty-two. World War I is about to begin. It will be carnage. At that moment, both Stein and Picasso have made a new language for their century. It is incredible to believe that is true. She is American. He is Spanish. They made it in Paris.

'I well remember at the beginning of the war,' Gertrude Stein wrote in 1938, 'being with Picasso on the Boulevard Raspail when the first camouflaged truck passed. It was at night, we had heard of camouflage, but we had not seen it and Picasso, amazed, looked at it and then cried out, yes it is we who made it, that is Cubism.'

Stein had published Tender Buttons, her collection of prose poems, or what she later described as verbal still lifes. Written between 1911 and 1912, maybe later, it is divided into three parts: Objects, Food, Rooms. She plays very precisely with the limits of language. Disturbs all literal associations and meanings. It is domestic and it is tense and it is made with cadence. Intense cadence.

'ROAST BEEF.
In the inside there is sleeping, in the outside there is reddening, in the morning there is meaning, in the evening there is feeling. In the evening there is feeling. In feeling anything is resting, in feeling anything is mounting, in feeling there is resignation, in feeling there is recognition, in feeling there is recurrence and entirely mistaken there is pinching.'

At that moment in 1914, Picasso had not only invented cubism alongside Braque, 'two mountaineers roped together inventing an artistic language', he had also assembled his first cardboard guitar and another one from sheet metal. These three-dimensional cubist objects are something between painting and sculpture. A revolution.

Stein and Picasso had made a new language. The door was no long ajar between the nineteenth and twentieth centuries. They had broken the chain and opened the door.

A year earlier, in 1913, Marcel Duchamp had made his way to a department store in the Marais, the BHV (Bazar de l'Hôtel de Ville), to purchase a bicycle wheel. He returned to his studio, turned the wheel upside down and attached it to a wooden stool. He had composed his first ready-made, removing the object from its context and function. Duchamp's bicycle wheel is a poem and an object, or a poetic object. He was twenty-five. Removing the object from its context and function is what Gertrude Stein was attempting to do with words in Tender Buttons. She was way ahead of her time as she always knew, bent over her desk, writing through the night in the shadow and light of two gas lamps.

In 1914 electricity was installed for the first time at 27 Rue de Fleurus.

17

Salvador Dalí regarded Duchamp as 'so detached' that sometimes he felt he 'was talking to his shadow'.

'He had the cold eye of his "ready-mades" and my Catalan passion had little tolerance for his sovereign indifference.'

The Unspeakable Confessions of Salvador Dalí (1976)

Gertrude Stein did not possess 'sovereign indifference'.

In 1914, much of her early writing remained unpublished. With Alice B.'s help she had self-published Three Lives, in 1912.

She was devastated and discouraged, but she did not take to her bed, like Alice James.

Deborah Levy

'In the midst of writing.
In the midst of writing there is merriment.'
  Lifting Belly (1915–17) by Gertrude Stein

18

On 12 November 2024, I was tipped off my bicycle by a taxi on the Rue de Rivoli. The driver told me I was not seriously hurt and then drove off. A waiter from one of the restaurants brought me a glass of water and lifted my bicycle on to the pavement. He pointed vaguely at my face and told me I was seriously hurt. He found my phone and asked me who to call.

The second person to be with me at the roadside was Fanny. She was holding a spare bicycle helmet in her hand and she was furious.

'Why are you cycling without a helmet on a main road in Paris? You're not on a country lane following the Loire, looking for castles and chateaux. Do we need a taxi or an ambulance?'

I could not speak because blood was dripping

from my lips. She dabbed at my lip with the napkin the waiter had given her.

'It's just a small cut,' she said, 'I'll walk you home.'

We returned to my studio in a taxi. In her left hand (phone always in her right hand) she held a small white box. Inside the box was a rum baba bouchon. Perched on top of the bouchon was a slice of roasted pineapple. She had queued for eight minutes to buy me the bouchon after the waiter had called her. She reckoned that if I was dead by the time she got to the Rue de Rivoli, she would eat the bouchon herself.

In fact, the waiter had told her I was looking on the road for one of my notebooks, so she, Fanny, reckoned that things were not that serious if Gertrude Stein was still on my mind. Scott Fitzgerald is Fanny's favourite American writer. While my lip continued to bleed, a stream of blood and not consciousness, she thought this was the right time to quote from The Great Gatsby: 'I wasn't actually in love, but I felt a sort of tender curiosity.'

That is apparently how she feels about

Nicole. Eva much prefers Nicole to Lucia but Fanny insists she can't truly love someone who hates coffee. Meanwhile, blood continued to flow from my lip while Fanny took a call from one of her clients. They were discussing the political situation in France and then moved on to the subject of a particular wine, which she thought was fresh but too light.

And then Fanny said, 'Yes, papa, it really is me,' and I realized she was talking to her father. Later, she told me her family knew that she would be staying in the grand empty house in the valley five miles from their home. Her father had made his way there the day before we arrived to hang a Chinese lantern in the pear tree. Its message was that she had burned too bright for her father in the fever of her adolescence, but his admiration for her was undimmed.

19

Eva and I swim together on Tuesdays at Piscine Pontoise, a pool near both our homes. When I told her about Fanny speaking to her father for the first time in decades, she wanted to know everything. I couldn't tell her everything because my lip was still swollen from the crash. Eva had brought me some sort of cream to rub into the bruises on my shins, knees and left arm. The cream smells like trees. Like winter. Like pain. I am also limping since the accident. In the water I am much faster than Eva. It is a struggle for her to get to the end of the pool without hanging on to the side halfway. I reckon she is also hanging on to the side in the situation with her husband in America. Since my bicycle accident, she is now worried that her cat might have been run over and that someone tipped it into a bin. Sometimes she's in tears about it.

What is it?

She confessed that when Fanny and I were in Avignon she had stood under a calming and gracious tree in the Parc des Buttes-Chaumont in the 19th arrondissement. Her first thought was that she would like to die in that tree. So she took out her phone and sent a photo of it to Hamish. No words. Just a photo of the tree. He texted back to say there were beautiful forests in Seattle, but if it came to it, he would like to die with her in that tree in Paris.

'And did you tell him that he had read your original thought?'

'You will have to speak to me in a language that is not English if you want that conversation,' she said. 'Try Danish, Spanish, French, and maybe even German.'

It is kind of Eva to slow down her own walking energies to adapt to my pace. And because I often talk to her about Gertrude Stein, she says, 'Yes, I walk alongside you and not ahead of you, but I am the genius, and you are not.' She knows that Gertrude Stein said of her brother, 'It was I who was the genius, there was no reason for it but I was, and he was not.' Eva always pokes me about how little I reveal about myself, even in the English language.

'I mean you might be a genius but I don't know anything about you.'

It's true that I hide from Eva's blinding blue gaze.

I had glanced at one of her drawings for her graphic novel and noted a character in her story who resembled myself. She was wearing a fur hat and carrying a suitcase in her right hand. Her left hand was pointing to a burst water pipe on the pavement. When I looked down the page I saw her (me) now up to her chin in the water leaking from the pipe. Perhaps I was wading through the streams of consciousness with a suitcase? One of Fanny's lovers, an actress who was very competitive and successful and who still lived in the road she grew up in and who always sounded angry, even when she said ordinary things, had called me deracinated.

I had to look it up.

After our swim we returned to Eva's studio to cook salmon for dinner. Eva poured something called mörk syrup into a bowl, dipped what looked like a paintbrush into the syrup and began to coat the fish in it. Apparently, mörk was a kind of molasses made from sugar beets. I could see the way she enjoyed the slow strokes of the brush across the silver skin of the fish. She had gravitas, authority, her feet apart, gripping the floor, her sad blue eyes, Owww, focused on the fish as her hand moved back and forth, and then she turned the fish over and began painting it in mörk all over again. I thought about her graphic novel and how she drew and painted all night but rarely showed me her work. I'd had to steal a glance, it was not offered. It's odd to have a friendship in which, apart from my thoughts on Gertrude Stein, I do not share what most preoccupies me. This is a new way of being and I quite enjoy it.

What is it? This new way of being? That is a question Eva never asks me.

   She had told me that in her graphic novel there was a chapter on her mother, who she drew in profile. That is how Eva saw her mother, always from the side. Her mother was a diplomat. The family moved around the world all the time, so maybe her mother was hard to catch. She had also begun to make posters to find her cat. Three of them were laid out on the floor. The word LOST painted in red and black letters at the top of the paper.

Deracinated.

It meant having no roots. Pulled up by the roots. Being rootless. It wasn't quite what Stein meant when she wrote 'There is no there there' to describe her childhood home in California after it was demolished. When describing Paul Cézanne's paintings, she observed that 'Everything was always there, really there . . .'

There is no there there. Would that be me? And Eva? Less so of Fanny, though it seems she had been un-belonged by those she had belonged to for many years.

Hamish was absent but there.
    Where?
    Paris.
    Gertude Stein was absent but there.
    Where?
    America.

Gertrude and Alice identified as Americans. They did not return to live in America, except for when Gertrude travelled there for her book tour of The Autobiography of Alice B. Toklas. No, she did not return to live in America, even though she was invited to tea with Eleanor Roosevelt at the Whitehouse. Not even when her name was up in lights. Not even, in Scott Fitzgerald's words, when she was going to be 'hymned and sung' in the country of her birth. In 1934 Fitzgerald wrote Stein a letter from Baltimore:

    'You were the same fine fire to everyone who sat on your hearth – for it was your hearth, because you carry home with you where ever you are – a home before which we have all always warmed ourselves.'

Dreams of Youth: The Letters of F. Scott Fitzgerald (2011), ed. Andrew Turnbull

Did he mean her writing was the hearth?

Or that she was hospitable to Americans passing through Paris in the 1920s? Or that she carried America with her wherever she landed?

Alice B. and Gertude did not return to America when the Germans occupied France in 1940. They holed up in the darkest days of Vichy in their rented house in the French countryside. Alice B. planted vegetables and Gertrude did nothing, often with their little dog sleeping across her shoulders and the big white poodle on her lap. The house was a rented chateau in Billignin, near Belley in the Auvergne-Rhône-Alpes region.

How did these two Jewish queer women and their collection of art survive the war? After all, it would have been perceived as 'degenerate' by the Nazis, who had set about destroying modernist art. Banishing it from public and private collections, harassing and belittling the artists, dismissing them from teaching positions and attacking the academic programmes of distinguished universities. Many of these academic institutions adapted to the Nazi ideological agenda. Picasso's work in private collections was seized, as was that of Georg Grosz, Van Gogh, Otto Dix – all modernist art was the enemy.

Why was it degenerate?

It had lost it.

Lost what?

Representation. Naturalism. Nostalgia. Obedience. Conformity. Certainty.

It was immoral, it was 'how sick minds viewed nature', it weakened the values of the Fatherland. It was ambiguous. Bold. It was fragmented and disorientating and it had been made by displaced artists who were deracinated. Gertrude and Alice had a friend who collaborated with the Vichy regime. He was a queer Catholic fascist with avant-garde tastes who admired Gertrude Stein's writing and even translated The Making of Americans into French. Bernard Faÿ protected them. Gertrude and Alice had first met Faÿ in 1924 and he became a lifelong friend. He gave Gertrude some strategies for how to deliver lectures to various audiences on her book tour in America. When he was appointed head of the Bibliothèque Nationale during the occupation he would have been a powerful and useful person to turn to for support.

Presumably Faÿ's sexual preferences were in hiding too, except with his lesbian friends, Gertrude and Alice. It must have been a relief for them all to talk freely. Did they talk freely? Who knows, but it must have been understood. His support provided coal. Rations. Driving privileges. Bread. When the Nazis turned up at Stein's Paris apartment to seize her art collection, Picasso apparently phoned Faÿ. The Gestapo tried on a few of Stein's Chinese jackets and some objects went missing, but they left the paintings undisturbed.

Eva is listening to all this as she steams the salmon.

'What would you have done, in their situation?' she asks me.

'I would have returned to America. I could never hang out with a man like Bernard Faÿ and feel entirely safe. Maybe he put pressure on Stein to translate Pétain's speeches into English.'

'Didn't her family tell her to come back?'

'I don't know. They were officially advised to go to Switzerland.'

Eva had trimmed her fringe again in the mirror that morning. It was very straight, symmetrical, just above her eyebrows. She had a steady hand. On the finger of her right hand was her wedding ring.

'It's one thing to write about these choices and another thing to live them,' Eva suggested. 'They must have been frightened. And the neighbours in their village obviously protected them.'

'Gertrude got on with everyone.'

Eva had returned to the kitchen, so I was shouting now. 'Left-wing, right-wing, she charmed them all. Like Raclette.'

I had hung our wet swimming costumes to dry on the radiator.

'Is that a good thing?' Eva wanted to know.

Someone was knocking on the door.

We hoped it wasn't Bernard Faÿ.

Fanny has joined us for dinner, unannounced. She had sex with Lucia on the floor near the rocking horse while the pug slept (Fanny is always very precise), between five and seven, and they set off with the pug for oysters afterwards and then Lucia, as usual, had to go and they parted, making no plans. Lucia liked to keep things vague.

Eva tells Fanny that when Matisse came round to Gertrude and Alice's home, uninvited, the cook suggested she would make him two fried eggs, not an omelette. They were the same ingredients, but Matisse would understand that fried eggs were a sign of disrespect because he was impolite to just turn up to be fed.

'So are you going to make me a fried egg?' Fanny wants to know.

'No.'

'Any luck with Bob?'

'Why did you choose such a stupid name? It's like my cat is wearing a baseball cap now.'

'I have some very cool baseball caps.' Fanny obviously feels bad about renaming it. 'My favourite is the one with EVA written across it.' She reached for a cigarette tucked into her belt and then walked into the kitchen to light it from the gas hob. 'Shall we meet over the weekend and organize a search party to find it?'

I explained that I could not commit to a date yet. I would be returning to Père Lachaise cemetery to look for Gertrude Stein's grave. Fanny is not interested in Gertrude Stein and thinks her knitted woollen stockings would have been erotically catastrophic. I was shocked to hear myself say out loud, 'I'm mostly interested in her wife and partner, Alice B. Toklas, with whom she was entwined for forty years.'

'I believe in polyamory,' Fanny said.

'Yes, you believe in polyamory, Fanny.' I reached towards her belt to pluck the second cigarette tucked inside it. 'But Alice B. was more honest than you. She was jealous of anyone who had sexual feelings for Gertrude. She was jealous of Gertrude's feelings for women before they even met, and she was jealous of Ernest Hemingway because she knew he was attracted to Gertrude.'

Fanny looked interested for the first time. She lit my cigarette for me and then waved her hand like a traffic cop to suggest I continue driving down this particular road. Preferably wearing a helmet.

'Men were not Gertrude's preference, but maybe she enjoyed the electricity of his desire. He wanted to take off her knitted stockings for sure. She was godmother to his son Bumby and wore a hat to the christening.'

'O-kaay,' Fanny said. 'If I had to choose between Stein and Hemingway I would go for Greta Garbo.'

*

Just before my bicycle accident I had walked into a bookshop and on the table were A Moveable Feast by Hemingway and The Autobiography of Alice B. Toklas by Stein. The way the books were arranged, lying across each other, made it look like Hemingway and Stein were drinking beer in a bathtub together. Who would have bought the beers? He was broke and often went hungry when he came to Paris in his twenties to try and make it as a writer. Stein had a moderate monthly allowance from the trust fund, and, as their friend Braque pointed out, he hoped that when he was rich, he too would employ a cook to make soufflé. Hemingway would have bought the beer. Stein was busy with her brother Leo buying the early work of Picasso, Cézanne and Matisse. She told him that if she had a choice between buying clothes or art, her choice was art. She gave him good advice about his writing. It was very attractive writing.

'When we came back to Paris it was clear and cold and lovely. The city had accommodated itself to winter, there was good wood for sale at the wood and coal place across our street, and there were braziers outside of many of the good cafés so that you could keep warm on the terraces ... The trees were sculpture without their leaves when you were reconciled to them, and the winter winds blew across the surfaces of the ponds and the fountains blew in the bright light.'

    A Moveable Feast (1964)

Typing out Hemingway is easier than typing out Stein.

    'A BOX.
    Out of kindness comes redness and out of rudeness comes rapid same question, out of an eye comes research, out of selection comes painful cattle.'

    Tender Buttons

Fanny has become concerned about how much time I spend alone typing out Stein's sentences. Why don't I read Michel Foucault instead? Or at least buy a new hat? Or even light a candle at Notre-Dame? Or make an appointment for an X-ray to check out why I am still limping after the accident? She thinks Gertrude Stein is depressing me. It's true that Gertrude transmits some sort of misery to me. The exhaustion of reading her prose. The never getting to the it of it. Somehow, it is my destiny to defend her.

When I told Fanny I like reading books I don't understand, she said, 'Why not have some sex you don't understand?'

Alice B. once quipped, after Stein had hogged all the conversation at a dinner party, 'Tonight Gertrude has said things it will take her years to understand.' I have been reading the first ninety pages of The Making of Americans for two years. There are one thousand pages. Eva is now on page seven hundred and ninety. She is the faster reader, I am the faster swimmer. Virginia Woolf couldn't 'brisk herself up' to get through it either when it was sent to her publishing house, the Hogarth Press.

*

'Every one then has in their living repeating, repeating of every kind of thing in them, repeating of the kind of impatient feeling they have in them, of the anxious feeling almost every one has more or less always in them.'

The Making of Americans

Fanny has no respect for Gertrude Stein. 'The repetition drives me in-saane. In France we like a clean sentence.' She stubbed her cigarette out on the red sole of her stiletto shoe and waited for me, as usual, to defend her.

'I think Stein once suggested, "There is no such thing as repetition. Only insistence."'

'I don't care about her insistence. No, I prefer our very own Gaston Bachelard. He speaks to me like your American expatriate between the wars could never speak.'

'Sometimes adolescence upsets everything. Adolescence, that fever of time in the human life! The memories are too clear for the dreams to be great. And the dreamer knows very well that he must go beyond the time of fevers to find the tranquil time, the time of the happy childhood inside his own substance.'

The Poetics of Reverie: Childhood, Language, and the Cosmo (1960) by Gaston Bachelard

She walked into the kitchen to help Eva clean the clams. Somewhere in the room with us, but not there in realism, was the Chinese lantern hanging from the pear tree near Avignon. Eva had told me that when she insisted Fanny let her mother know she would be visiting the grand empty villa near their home, Fanny had said, 'O-kaay, I will make the call and then cry all over my pug, who is allergic to tears as well as moonlight.'

When Fanny walked back to pick up her phone, I told her that the philosopher Jacques Derrida had been very interested in Stein.

'We have plenty of excellent writers of our own, including Derrida. Marguerite Duras knew how to use a comma, so did Balzac. If you excuse me I need to do some admin now.'

I watched her swiping and messaging. Her body was still with us, but she had clearly left the room for more interesting universes.

After a while, she looked up at me from the screen. 'Are you not interested in some companionship in your life?' It was as if she was suggesting I was writing an essay on Stein to fill a hole in my life.

'The problem is that men my age are intolerable. I am required to listen to them speak for the duration of our encounter but they never ask me any questions about my own life. There are a few exceptions. These exceptions are incredible men. They are so rare we must treat them like snow leopards.'

Eva walked in carrying a tray on which three bowls of rice, clams and fish were arranged. She sat on the floor.

'I don't believe you will find a snow leopard on Fanny's dating app.'

Fanny disagreed. 'Be your formidable self on your profile and you might find a snow leopard.'

Eva wanted to know if Fanny would like to

borrow her copy of The Making of Americans. 'I can lend it to you over the weekend.'

'No. I don't want to work so hard for so little reward.'

'Yes, that's what I feel about dating a man of my age,' I chimed in. Fanny was still scrolling and tapping on her dating app. She leaned over to see if I approved of where she had placed the full stops in her message on the app.

Sex. Possibly.

'What is it that makes sex possible?' she asked me.

Eva and I exchanged judging glances. Wasn't Fanny supposed to be in love with Lucia? What about their co-owned pug, who hated moonlight?

We started to eat the salmon and clams. Eva had cooked the rice in the broth from the clams. Meanwhile, Fanny was tapping her phone with one hand and pouring soy sauce on her rice with the other. I thanked Eva for putting together such a tasty dish at the last moment. It was her father's recipe. Eva had grown up in Copenhagen so there was always an abundance of fish for her father's recipes. He collected them from the New York Times, though her mother preferred a sandwich. When Eva told me she would like to illustrate my essay on Gertrude Stein, Fanny threw her phone to the floor.

It landed under the table in the exact place Eva's cat had always slept.

After a while, Eva reached for a soft pencil and began sketching Fanny. 'You did not say what it is that makes sex possible.'

Gertrude Stein had asked this question to her aunts in Baltimore in her teens. What is it that makes sex possible? She lived with them after her parents died, before she went to college. She reported back to her brother Leo that these women found sexual intercourse 'not satisfying, and they don't want it'.

'Listening is what makes sex possible.'

'Did you say listening?'

'Yes,' I replied. 'Really listening.'

'Maybe that's for love.' Fanny looked perturbed. 'It can be a turn-off in sex.'

'Why?'

'If we really understood the person we are having sex with we would run away as fast as possible.'

It was the first time we had seen Eva smile since her cat disappeared.

Fanny's hair was particularly glossy that evening. Eva reached out and touched the ends with her fingertips.

'Lucia is a total mess. Why don't you just settle for Nicole. I like the way she always checks if your glass at the table is empty. Water or wine, she fills your glass. And I like the way she sings along with the radio in a taxi.'

Fanny reached for the third cigarette tucked into her belt.

'So thank you for your advice, Eva. It's me who is the total mess and Lucia is totally together. But tomorrow is my day off so we could do our night search for Bob.'

Eva still leaves her door ajar on the chain in case it comes back.

The chain has not been broken. The half-open door is poised between her past with

Hamish and her present life. Fanny thinks our friend has nothing to lose but her chain, yet I'm not so sure. Meanwhile, rain was falling gently on Paris, including on all its trees and statues and on every caress at a bus stop and on every kiss by a fountain.

20

Stein wrote Lifting Belly between 1915 and 1917. A long poem about making love to Alice, it will remain unpublished until after her death.

'Lifting belly is so kind.
Lifting belly fattily.
Doesn't that astonish you.
You did want me.'

Bee Time Vine: And Other Pieces, 1913–1927 (1953), ed. Virgil Thomson

21

Ulysses had been banned in America for obscenity and Sylvia Beach was going to publish it. Founder in 1919 of the first Shakespeare and Company, an English-language bookshop and lending library in Paris, Sylvia Beach was a woman of steely courage and intoxicating charm. I can imagine her hiding in the broom cupboard when Gertrude Stein walked into her bookshop. Stein was devastated that Sylvia had not published The Making of Americans, which had been lying in a drawer like an unclaimed suicide since 1911. Sylvia's mother had lent her the money to start the bookshop. She lived frugally and loved writers but did not want to be a writer, though she wrote very well.

Gertrude did not have to work for a living. She could do what she liked. She and Alice cancelled their subscription to the library and joined the American Library across the river instead. Sylvia published Ulysses and it nearly bankrupted her. Her bookshop, which was also a meeting place for broke and hungry writers, had a different mood from the Stein salon. I can't see Sylvia Beach preparing a lecture on the formal and thematic strategies put to work in various novels and delivering it to the transient readers who used the shop and library. She loaned French francs to the American writers waiting for their dollars to arrive and allowed them to use the address of her bookshop as a post-office box while they moved apartments, fell in love and out of love, starved and feasted. She was excited by the thought that some of them were maniacs, talented and untalented. Sylvia Beach was loved rather than admired or feared.

When Joyce and Stein finally met they spoke briefly about living near each other in Paris. They had both travelled a long way from home. Joyce had left Ireland in 1904, Stein had left America in 1903. They had lost it. What is it?

Ireland and America. Yet, that's what they wrote about in Ulysses and The Making of Americans. Ireland and America.

James Joyce wrote about Dublin in Trieste, Zurich and Paris.

Gertrude Stein wrote about America with all the rhapsody of Walt Whitman while living at 27 Rue de Fleurus in Paris, a five-minute walk from the Luxembourg Gardens with its statues, fountains, fruit trees and orchids.

'In the summer it was good for generous sweating to help the men make the hay into bails for its preserving and it was well for ones growing to eat radishes pulled with the black earth sticking to them and to chew the mustard and find roots with all kinds of funny flavors in them, and to fill ones hat with fruit and sit on the dry ploughed ground and eat and think and sleep and read and dream and never hear them when they would all be calling . . .'
The Making of Americans

22

Fanny and Eva have bought two torches at our local tabac on Boulevard Saint-Germain near Place Maubert. There had been a long queue, Eva said, mostly people buying lottery tickets. And a tourist in front of her who needed batteries for her radio. No one could work out why she had a radio that only worked with batteries. When she was questioned, she said, 'Why do you think there will always be electricity? When I travel I carry my little radio, a power bank and cash.'

At the Vietnamese cafe next door, our friend Julian was wrapping a summer roll in a leaf of lettuce. He had very delicate hands. Julian was keen to tell us some important news about his rendezvous, which was to take place after he had eaten the solitary summer roll. It involved an attempt at seduction. He was nervous but determined, which was why he was having a light dinner rather than the heavier lacquered duck with sticky rice, which was his preference. We confirmed that his hair looked good and his beard perfectly trimmed. Eva suggested he soften his lips with her lip balm. She even offered him a splash of her industrial cologne.

Like the rise of fascism everywhere, the pigeons were out in full. The cranes restoring Notre-Dame were now resting in the sky. No one murmured Awww when they gazed into Eva's blue eyes, but they wanted to. She was tense about the night search for her cat, but like Julian she was determined to capture love and hold it in her arms. The men sleeping rough around Place Maubert were now sitting with their backs against the walls of various cashpoints at the three banks nearby. At the boulangerie across the road, the woman who Julian was planning to seduce was buying a Mont Blanc, a pastry made with candied chestnuts, chestnut puree and almond crème. It was topped with whipped cream to suggest the summit of a snow-capped mountain. When Fanny spotted her in the queue, we hoped that she would climb to the summit of erotic pleasure with Julian and enjoy the mountain air.

Eva wore white clogs for the night search. Fanny asked her if she knew the Industrial Revolution was over and there were no longer textile mills and mines that required workers to wear this particular protective footwear. Eva closed her blue eyes. We stared at her pale face now unlit by her startling gaze. It was as if the lights had been switched off in France, Belgium and Luxembourg. Her lips were moving and we wondered if she was praying. And then she opened her eyes and told us she was ready to begin the search for it. Fanny wore black leather riding boots and sunglasses, though it was dark in Paris at five in the afternoon in November. As we made our way to the Quai de la Tournelle, we noticed that Eva had already stapled some of the trees with the posters she had made to tell Paris about her missing cat. The word LOST floated at the top of the paper. Beneath it, she had painted her cat inside a small black square. It was somewhat cubist in design, two colours, red and black. One ear tiny, the other ear taller, both triangles outlined in red. It was not how it looked, it was how she thought about her cat; it was how her cat was seen by her. Bob came across as strangely mischievous and regal. Eva had also created a new email address so that if it was found by someone, they could contact her. She told us her cat didn't feel like Bob so she wasn't even going there. Nowhere on the poster was the name Bob, and she quoted Gertrude Stein to me.

'I like the feeling of words doing as they want to do and as they have to do.'

Eva seemed to agree with Stein all the time.

I had made gazpacho, which I transferred to a plastic bowl and sellotaped a lid on top of it. Fanny, always the contrarian, had no respect for the endeavour of pulverizing tomatoes, garlic and peppers. 'Can I remind our English friend that gazpacho is a cold soup for summer in Spain. It is November. We are in Paris. How are we supposed to eat soup on a nocturnal hunt for a cat? We don't know where Bob will lead us.'

Across the road was the Seine and Notre-Dame. Fanny was clear that it was useless to stand on the banks of the river and call for a cat. There were too many places to hide. Eva had strange logic on this matter. 'We must stand by a barge because fish shelter under the boats and my cat will be hungry and see the fish.'

'O-kaay,' Fanny performed an eye roll, 'we will stand by one barge only and you will choose which one and you will do the calling.' Fanny tended to give the orders. She had more sex than we did and this gave her energy and authority. We stood on either side of Eva when she found her barge and we were at her side when she called across the Seine, 'It, it, it, come home.'

It was lost.

It was having something to live for.

I thought a lot about Eva in her white clogs at this moment.

*

After a while, Fanny whispered to me that this was like the end of the world. She could feel herself disintegrating. Eva had clearly lost it.

Frankly, she, Fanny, did not want to be seen calling for a lost cat across the waters of the Seine. One of her clients in the world of finance might see her and this person would be right to question her judgement about managing their wealth. We gazed at Eva, who seemed to believe that her cat could sense her love and that this love was so powerful it would hear her call and wherever it was it would run towards her love.

What do we have to lose to become modern?
Shame.

After a while, Fanny pushed Eva across the road towards a small public garden called Square Danielle Mitterrand. She pointed to an elderly man sitting on a green wooden bench and steered Eva in his direction. He was smartly dressed, a walking stick perched near his knees. We asked him if he had seen a cat and described Bob in some detail. Eva even told him that her cat's name was it, his tail was black but the tip was white. He listened and then said, 'I am only here for fifteen minutes to inhale the Mexican orange blossom, a shrub that someone inspired has planted in this garden.' He pointed to the remaining creamy-white flowers on a shrub opposite the bench.

'It still has a few flowers in November,' he told us mournfully, 'but they might fall if it gets too cold.' He invited us to join him and inhale the Mexican orange blossom. We all sat in silence on the green curved bench with him and inhaled the blossom. After a while, I handed him the plastic container of gazpacho I had made earlier.

'It's a cold soup,' I said.

He took the spoon and tasted it.

'Well, I do believe this is a gazpacho. This has completed the joy of the winter flowering.'

Eva told him it was a recipe from The Alice B. Toklas Cook Book, 1954. A gazpacho from Seville. Alice B. also had recipes for gazpacho from Malaga, Cordoba and Segovia. She explained to him that I was writing an essay about Gertrude Stein, and then added experimentally, 'I am her assistant. In fact, it is likely that I will illustrate the pages if she ever writes it. At the moment we are reading The Making of Americans. It is a history of a family over three generations,' and then she told him that another identifying mark on her cat was that its right ear was smaller than its left. Much smaller. The size of the smallest human toe.

He promised to look out for it, in fact he had taken out his pen and appeared to be taking notes in a small red diary, but then he tore out the page and handed it to me. It seemed to be a phone number. And his address. Underneath his address, which was in Montmartre, he had written his name. Jean-Luc.

'Madame,' he said, 'perhaps I can invite you to dine with me, in return for Alice Babette Toklas's gazpacho from Seville.'

I was touched he knew the B. between Alice and Toklas was for Babette. Alice was often described as ugly or brittle or her looks were described as 'Semitic'. When she was young her curls reached beyond her shoulders. I found her very recognizable.

Rain started to fall on the 5th arrondissement. The fragrance of Mexican orange blossom was intense in the rain.

'I like Paris in November,' he said. 'It is calm.'

A wind blew in from the Seine. 'It is reassuring to know,' Jean-Luc continued, 'that in a time of uncertainty, one thing is certain. The Seine will always flow into the English Channel between Le Havre and Honfleur.'

'Well, so-rry to rain on your river,' Fanny interrupted his reverie, 'all the rivers in the world are dying, so it is not a certainty at all.'

'But your rain will be very healthy for my river,' he replied, and before Fanny returned to flood sewage into his river, he turned to Eva.

'I saw the posters on the trees. There are people and animals I miss too. I hope the search ends well for you.'

He tussled with the sprig of Mexican orange blossom he had plunged through the buttonhole of his coat and held it out to her, as if in condolence. Eva thanked him and tucked it behind her ear. At that moment we heard something move through the bush behind us. Eva gasped and touched the ends of her fringe. It moved again and then stopped. Fanny shone her torch into the leaves. Eva was now tiptoeing towards the bush. Jean-Luc stood up and grabbed his walking stick. He seemed very keen to find Eva's cat as he made his way towards the bushes. He parted his lips and made shpp shpp shpp noises. A rat ran through the flowering Mexican orange blossom tree. We thought he was going to whack the rat with his stick, but it remained still in his hand. He told us it was a pleasure to make our acquaintance and he hoped the missing cat would return to its home. His eyes were on Eva as he spoke.

Later, on the walk back to Rue des Trois Portes, Fanny said, 'We found a cat, just not the right one. I think we have found your snow leopard. And he is your age, maybe a little older, I know it.'

'How do you know it?'

She paused, searching for the cigarette she had tucked into her belt.

'You both have well-lived faces.'

At last she found her lighter.

Alice B. loved to smoke cigarettes in all weathers, mostly untipped Pall Malls. She planted tobacco in their garden in Bugey during the war. When she tried to give up in old age her plan was to only smoke *tipped* Pall Malls. I reminded Fanny that cigarettes were sold to women in the 1920s as 'torches of freedom'. 'Yes,' Fanny said, 'when I smoke I am living my truth. Today I bought silk lingerie and I thought, Is this for me or is it for Lucia or Nicole or Martine or is it for freedom or is it for your essay on Gertrude Stein?' She tapped her phone. Fanny was always handling some kind of investment for one of her customers. Working with clients in different time zones meant she sometimes had very little sleep. She offered her cigarette to Eva, who lifted her hand to say no to the torch of freedom. Eva was silent and moody. Under the moonlight we glimpsed the posters on the trees, but could only see the word LOST because it was painted in capital letters. In the distance I saw Jean-Luc leaping on to the bridge at a brisk pace. He seemed not to need the help of his walking stick.

'How will I recognize him if we meet again?' I asked my friends.

'It was so dark, I hardly saw his face.'

Fanny tucked her lighter into her belt and then reached for Eva's hand.

'If you meet in a bar just do what Simone de Beauvoir did when she first met Sartre. Look for the ugliest man sitting alone.'

23

Gertrude Stein's science training is all there in her every sentence.

'Gertrude Stein, in her work, has always been possessed by the intellectual passion for exactitude in the description of inner and outer reality. She has produced a simplification by this concentration, and as a result the destruction of associational emotional emotion in poetry and prose. She knows that beauty, music, decoration, the result of emotion should never be the cause, even events should not be the cause of emotion nor should they be the material of poetry or prose. They should

consist of an exact reproduction of either an outer or an inner reality.'
The Autobiography of Alice B. Toklas

At Johns Hopkins she studied brain modelling and neurology.

24

I walked into the restaurant and recognized Jean-Luc immediately. His bulging green eyes were kind and startling. Miraculously, his silver hair was abundant, slicked down with some sort of gel, the collar and cuffs of his elegant white shirt were sharp and precise. He wore a green tie. Across his feet lay his walking stick. When he noticed I had noticed his stick, he stretched out his hand to take my own.

'Somehow it found me and will not leave.'

He had just returned from an auction of five of Rodin's sketches of Isadora Duncan, not that he could afford to buy one, he regretted, but it lifted his spirit to see Rodin's infatuated drawings of her dancing barefoot in flimsy Greek togas, ungirdled, unashamed and free. He stood up to carry my umbrella to a ceramic stand by the door. I noted his straight spine and graceful poise. He did not seem to need his stick. When he returned, he confessed he had asked his neighbour, a distinguished engineer, to give him some guidance for our meeting. What did his neighbour tell him?

'A strong sense of purpose is necessary to achieve the greatest possible success.'

'And what is your sense of purpose?' I asked.

'To eat well and have convivial conversation. And what about you?'

'I'm busy writing my essay on Gertrude Stein. Mostly working from her 1914 book of poetry, Tender Buttons.'

He tapped my hand with his fingers.

'Stein is referring to nipples,' he said. 'Tender to the touch. Most definitely. Let us share a bottle of wine.' After a brief consultation we ordered a Côtes du Rhône to accompany the pâté maison. It was dense and rich, perhaps made from chicken and duck livers.

'I think Stein just liked buttons,' I replied. 'She used to go to Bon Marché to buy them.'

The waiter came over to remove the walking stick from Jean-Luc's feet. He wanted to know if it would be agreeable with Monsieur if he were to place it in the stand with the umbrellas. Jean-Luc agreed, but insisted the walking stick would find him again, as if it were inclined to make its way back to his feet of its own accord. When we praised the pâté, the waiter told us the secret was to fry bacon rinds with onion and butter before adding the livers. Jean-Luc tapped my hand again. 'Back to your thoughts on Tender Buttons.'

'I think Stein was just referring to common household objects.'

He seemed displeased with my answer, searched his pocket and found a square of silk into which he thrust his nose and sneezed twice. 'Please excuse me,' he apologized. 'Do you have a favourite line in Tender Buttons?'

'Yes. "What is the wind, what is it."'

'Wind is the movement of air,' he replied.

I explained that Stein would have known that. She had a science training and possessed a scholarly grip on grammar, yet removed all question marks from her work because she said it was obvious when something is a question. She found them revolting. And she thought commas were servile. Readers should be free to take a breath whenever they felt like it. Her main aim was for a sentence to push onwards.

'A comma by helping you along holding your coat for you and putting on your shoes keeps you from living your life as actively as you should lead it . . .'

'Poetry and Grammar', in Lectures in America (1935) by Gertrude Stein

When the waiter returned, Jean-Luc asked him a question.

'What is the menu du jour, what is it?'

'Yes,' I interrupted, 'but . . . "What is the wind, what is it" could also be a meditation on something rather than a question, or it could be Alice B. farting.'

Jean-Luc looked appalled. 'The British love their farting jokes.'

'It's not a joke,' I replied, 'and I am not entirely British.'

'I know.'

'How do you know?'

'The author biography on some of your books gives this information.'

It was attractive that he did not press for more information.

The menu du jour was pot-au-feu. Carrots, parsnip, peppercorns, beef ribs, shank bones, oxtail. We ordered it. Jean-Luc wanted to know more about Eva's cat. I told him how Bob had always been present during Eva's weekly FaceTime with her husband in Seattle, but now it was missing they had both lost the will to keep to their weekly appointment.

'Well,' he said, 'it sounds like a ménage à trois between Bob, Eva and Hamish. Have you ever tried it?'

I was silent for a while.

'Fanny and Eva and me are à trois in friendship. We see each other at least twice a week and speak on the phone every day. For example, when

I asked Eva what she was drawing today, she said, "The angles of elbows and the tips of tongues." She is a graphic artist and sees the world visually.'

'I see.' Jean-Luc was now mashing a potato into the cup of broth that came with the pot-au-feu and in which the beef had been cooked. 'But now that her cat is missing, Eva and Hamish are, so to speak, à deux and not trois, nose to nose, without the distraction of Bob.'

I agreed this might be the case.

'It seems to me that Bob does all the feeling for Eva?'

'Well,' I replied, 'we could say that her feelings are feeling her even if she doesn't want to feel them. And the same could be said for Gertrude Stein, which is why she did not want to be understood. It is after all exposing to be understood.'

'And very tiring,' he murmured. 'I have been teaching American literature to fifteen-year-olds at various international schools for many years. I would prefer my students to risk not understanding. To leave my class bewildered but elated. Yet, there is the question of exams. To polish understanding with the soiled cloth of clarity has been my destiny and my horror.'

It was very convivial to speak to Jean-Luc in a warm restaurant in the 11th arrondissement on a cold November night. The glass globe above our heads spun a warm golden light across the white tablecloths. I suggested that Bob might have run away to Seattle to be with Hamish, preferring deux to trois.

'I think it is birds rather than cats who make that sort of long journey,' he replied. 'The migration of birds across vast distances has always thrilled me. The endurance of it. Flying through the night, taking advantage of tailwinds. Especially the small birds that cross the open seas.'

He tapped my hand yet again. He seemed to be fond of this gesture. 'And why are you so interested in Eva's search for her cat?'

'I don't quite understand it,' I confessed, 'but I have decided to throw myself into it and see where it takes me. Fanny, who is a genius, renamed Eva's cat. She called it Bob in an attempt to make it a cat again.'

'You've lost me,' Jean-Paul murmured.

'I hope not,' I replied. 'I have only just found you.'

Our eyes met and we held the gaze.

'Where did she get Bob from?'

'Her landlord was moving to Lyon and asked if she wanted his cat, which she did.'

'I see.' He tapped my hand again. 'I am beginning to comprehend the composition of your essay. You will write about the avant-garde in the language of realism. The push and pull of both constituencies will be confronting. Realism and the avant-garde both have high humidity, yet I'm sure you're discovering they behave very differently when exposed to direct sunlight.'

Fortunately, the waiter came over to give us some information about the pot-au-feu. It was cooked for six hours by the establishment's new chef from Burgundy. He had decided to add leeks at the last moment and was keen to elicit our opinion. We agreed the leeks were a perfect combination with the peppercorns. The waiter seemed satisfied and walked off to collect a plate of haddock and poached egg for the mayor, who was sitting nearby.

'May I ask why you are so preoccupied with Eva?' Jean-Luc's knees were now touching my knees, which were still tender from the bicycle accident. The small movement he had made to achieve this new intimacy was somehow inspiring. I had not even noticed he was edging closer to my bruised knees. It was as if he had crossed the very busy intersection of my resistance by invisibly levitating over the traffic.

'Oh, I'm obsessed with Fanny too. Gertrude Stein knew Matisse, Picasso and Braque, but I am more interested in Fanny and Eva. Everyone already knows about Picasso, but no one knows about Eva.'

'Well, what do you know about Eva?' He dabbed a few drops of broth from his lips with the square of silk.

'Not much. She married Hamish when she was nineteen.' I filled up both our glasses with the Côtes du Rhône. 'But then I know very little about Gertrude Stein, even though I have read some of her books and many more books about her. But what I do know about Eva is she likes to paint sharon fruit perilously perched on her window ledge, it's also known as a persimmon, she can barely swim but somehow keeps afloat, she suggests that if World War Three breaks out we take a morphine tablet and die together in the Alpine meadows of Switzerland, her preference is to use unscented goat's milk soap because it calms inflamed skin, her husband is elusive, a shadow man living far away, she is thin as a vine and washes her hair every day.'

'How so?'

'With water and shampoo,' I replied. 'Is that what you meant?'

'I think I meant how does she compare to Picasso.'

'I am not looking for equivalence. We could say that he was short and she is short and Alice Babette Toklas was under five foot.'

'Yes, it was a stupid question,' he said. 'Your French is very unusual and I'm feeling somewhat emotional. In fact, I feel estranged from myself. As if I am floating away for fear you might not wish to see me again.'

I suggested we land on the ground with a round of Calvados. Jean-Luc, who had at first appeared ugly to me, was now becoming alluring. He seemed to have landed and was knowledgeable but not portentous about American poetry.

While we talked about Frank O'Hara's Lunch Poems and the New York poets, his right knee pressed a little harder on the bruises of my own right knee. We agreed that we liked movies and chocolate sodas and cheeseburgers turning up in a poem and snow and traffic and Christmas trees and yoyos and a carpenter's pencil turning up in a poem and instant coffee and Rachmaninoff and Bastille Day and swimming and anxiety and cigarettes all turning up in a poem, which they do in the writing of Frank O'Hara. And we liked his poem 'À la Recherche d' Gertrude Stein', where he gets rid of punctuation so he can hurtle through the poem at greater speed towards his lover to speak directly about how all anxiety lifts when they are naked together and how entwined they stand a chance of defeating the enemies within themselves that stop them from loving more courageously.

Jean-Luc stared into the breadbasket.

'I too have been in love like that O'Hara poem,' he confessed. 'And yet love did not endure, we did not defeat the enemies within ourselves that slayed our courage.'

I suddenly felt that my life in La Ville Lumière had just begun.

I felt it with violence. The violence of hope.

Later we linked arms and he walked me home. 'You are a most convivial companion.' His voice was direct and endearing. 'In every way you are a woman I would like to get to know.' He touched my black fur hat. I leaned towards him and touched his green tie. He leaned towards me and softly kissed my eyes, which were closed, under the November rain. Perhaps he had dismantled the grammar of a kiss. When we arrived at the entrance of my building he seemed reluctant to leave and I wanted him to stay. We were calm and terrified. 'May I ask,' he whispered, 'if it is possible . . .' He looked up at the sky and then down at my hat.

'May I ask if it is possible for you to give me Eva's phone number?'

In the humiliation of the moment, I remembered he had requested that his neighbour give him guidance for our meeting. What did his neighbour tell him? 'A strong sense of purpose is necessary to achieve the greatest possible success.' He was still lingering while I pressed the digits of my door code. I wanted him to leave now, to float away, to be estranged from himself, to levitate above the Seine and make his way back to Montmartre. He called out my name, but I had already shut the door.

Yet, I was working with a strange intuition.
 To do with language. To do with listening.
 Something he had said in the restaurant stayed with me.

Back in my studio I had to pour a cool glass of water and try to catch his words. I emptied my mind so that whatever he had uttered could step into the space I had made for it. Maybe even dance barefoot into the empty space, like Rodin's sketch of Isadora dancing ungirdled and free. Gazing out of the window, I saw a woman struggle with her hire bike and phone. The app would not allow her to park and end the ride. It was raining of course. It is a terrible feeling not to be able to end something when the journey has been concluded. I knew this from my first marriage.

At last his words came back to me. They were to do with his walking stick, which he had placed across his feet.

'Somehow it found me and will not leave.'

That was the sort of thing that might be said of a cat who arrives out of the blue and decides to stay.

25

'What does literature do and how does it do it. And what does English literature do and how does it do it. If it describes what it sees how does it do it. If it describes what it knows how does it do it and what is the difference between what it sees and what it knows. And then too there is what it feels and then also there is what it hopes and wishes.'

'What is Literature', in Lectures in America

Obviously, all question marks had left the building and were smoking outside.

26

I told Eva that Jean-Luc had requested her telephone number. She seemed surprised, even scared, but then she took up a pencil and started to draw the interior of a house. 'I wonder why he wants to talk with me.' She looked down at her bare feet and started to rotate her ankles in small circles.

'How was your evening with him, by the way?'

On her shelf was a tiny glass vase filled with water. It could fit into my hand. And inside it was the sprig of Mexican orange blossom that Jean-Luc had picked for her on the night we searched for it. She started to draw a low table and a small wooden lamp.

'Yes,' she eventually said, 'tell him he can find me on WhatsApp.' She flipped her fringe out of her blue eyes. Perhaps, in Malcolm X's words, she was a blue-eyed devil.

'I have lost it, but you have found your snow leopard.'

'He is not a snow leopard at all,' I replied. 'That would be to misunderstand the rare species I was referring to.'

I took out my phone and texted her number to Jean-Luc. Eva had now sketched a row of coat hooks spaced on the wall of the entrance of the house she was drawing.

As I walked down the stairs, I couldn't be sure, but I thought I could hear Eva crying.

'All of the sadness of the city came suddenly with the first cold rains of winter . . .'
A Moveable Feast

27

In her most brilliant moment, Gertrude Stein describes the first time she travelled on an aeroplane during her American book tour for The Autobiography of Alice B. Toklas. She was now sixty and famous. The depressed, nameless young woman who had lurked in her brother Leo's shadow, had delivered around seventy-four lectures across thirty-seven states. She looked out of the window and was amazed to glimpse the geometry of the abstract shapes she saw below.

'I saw all the lines of cubism made at a time when not any painter had ever gone up in an airplane. I saw there on the earth the mingling lines of Picasso, coming and going, developing and destroying themselves, I saw the simple solutions of Braque, I saw the wandering lines of Masson, yes I saw and once more I knew that a creator is contemporary, he understands what is contemporary when the contemporaries do not yet know it . . .'

    Picasso by Gertrude Stein

Stein was startled that Picasso and Braque had seen something that existed in the world that was not yet visible to the human eye. Yet they had seen it. Cubism had made the invisible visible. That's what it takes to be modern. To see it first. And this first revelatory glimpse, she insisted, will always create art that is out of step with its time.

What did she want writing to do to her?
    She liked to read detective stories.

28

My essay on Gertrude Stein was going quite well until the mice arrived in my studio. Up to that moment it had been a calm place to write. Calm in solitude, calm in loneliness, in all weathers, in most regrets, what were they. As I was typing out some of Stein's writing a mouse ran across the room. It was the size of my thumb and then it seemed there were bigger shapes flickering over the floor. Under the sofa. Between the logs stacked by the fireplace, across the kilim rugs, behind the washing machine and the sink.

I called Fanny, who told me it was normal to host some mice in Paris. 'We live by the Seine,' she said. 'It was bound to happen.'

'But I can't live like this.'

'Then you will have to set traps with bait.'

I told her I couldn't handle wounded mice in the traps.

'Then you have to close the holes in the walls with wire wool.' She was shouting down the phone now. 'Look, there's bad shit happening in the world and you are going crazy about one mouse.'

Three mice.

I was scared they would crawl over me while I slept.

When Fanny finally arrived at my studio she had gathered her thoughts with the help of Eva to make some sort of pitch to me.

'The mouse symbolizes the mind. Ganesha is the Lord of the Intellect. Ganesha was often riding around on a mouse. You are an intellectual person, which means your mind is agile like the mice, so why don't you live peacefully together?' She thought it was obvious they could live peacefully with me. I should learn from Ganesha.

I made an appointment for a mouse catcher to come over the next morning. All night long there were mice in my mind. Flickering, running around. No, I did not ride on a mouse like Ganesha. The mice rode inside me. I was awake all night.

Visions of London stepped into the Paris night.

Red double-decker buses rumbling slowly down the bus lanes, windows steamed up in winter with the dust and grime of this ancient city under which lurks a Roman temple built to honour a bull-slaying god, the splendour of its trees, including the English oak with its harvest of autumnal acorns, the wildness in some of its parks, the foxes at night walking every neighbourhood, its residents carrying rucksacks, AirPods in ears, all of us fierce, wrecked, gentle, outraged, shy, extrovert and mostly patient in queues and under the rain clouds, working all hours to pay our bills and laughing at ourselves as the dark tidal Thames made its way towards the treacherous North Sea.

In the morning the mouse catcher was late. He had a lot of work on and I was lucky he could fit me in. He sat on the edge of the sofa and told me my options. Every now and again his head would suddenly jerk to the side as if he had seen something. Or he would put a hand to his ear as if he could hear the scuttling of rodents. His ears were large and the light shone through them. I began to think he was performing for me so he could raise the price of his services.

I needed to be deep in it so I wouldn't notice the mice.

What was it?

My essay on Gertrude Stein.

My studio was on the fifth floor of an ancient building. The mice might be distant relatives of rodents glimpsed by Rodin while his hands were deep in clay or wax or plaster. He was deep in it so he wouldn't have noticed. What I really needed was it.

What was it?

Love.

I needed to be deep in it.

'Let's not delay this any longer,' the mouse catcher told me, 'I will begin.' He was a big man, thick fingers, over which he slipped blue latex gloves. He started to place six little plastic burrows with a sachet of poison inside each one of them around my studio. Under the holes in the wall, next to a little grate in the wall, under a few wooden beams. He tiptoed around the kilims for thirty minutes, and then he lay on his stomach and peered under my bed. A hole was cut into each plastic burrow for the mice to scuttle into and inside these burrows they would nibble on the poison. It felt bad, but I couldn't live with the mice.

What is it?
   The wind, what is it.
   My mouse phobia, what is it?

That's what Fanny wants to know.

'O-kaay,' she said, when we met for a walk. 'It's as if one tiny mouse has unleashed all your anxieties from the past and your fears about the future. It is too small, this mouse, to carry such a weight on your behalf.'

'Three mice. They are sharing the burden.'

At the same time I was thinking about the moment the waiter had asked Jean-Luc's permission to place his walking stick in the stand with the umbrellas. Jean-Luc had insisted the walking stick would find him again, as if it were an animal inclined to make its way back to his feet. And I was thinking about Gertrude Stein's definition of intelligence as knowing something before you know it.

I knew something about it that I did not yet know.

We tried to discuss other things.

She put her arm around my shoulder and asked about my dinner with Jean-Luc. I told her he was more interested in Eva.

'I'm sorry,' she said. 'It does sound like that. After all, Eva is young, slim and beautiful and you are not.' She pretended to search for a cigarette tucked into her belt. 'But maybe he wants you both? Are you into a ménage à trois like he is?'

I shook my head, which was still full of the movement of mice.

'But perhaps you are in a ménage à trois with Gertrude and Alice? I mean, to write your essay you sort of have to be. Why not have an orgy?'

Drops of rain began to fall on the newly restored steeple of Notre-Dame. We could hear seagulls screeching somewhere. Across the bridge tourists were taking photos for Instagram on the terrace of a cafe decorated with fake cherry blossom.

'What you need in your studio is a cat,' Fanny said.

'Yes, I thought of that.'

I told Fanny that I believed Jean-Luc would lead us to Eva's cat.

I repeated for her his comment about the walking stick and my intuition that he was speaking to me through an object. She asked if I had his address. When I confirmed that I did, she suggested we take the Métro to Montmartre to visit him on 18 November.

'I believe this essay on Gertrude Stein is

pushing you to the edge of insanity. You are spending too much time alone in her company. Why not walk to that garden square and inhale the Mexican orange blossom?'

After a while I asked about her and Lucia's co-owned pug.

'It's like we have a child who only drinks coconut water and is scared of the moon,' she said.

To distract myself from the mice and thoughts from the past which the mice had delivered to me, also the sting of the Frank O'Hara poem about defeating the enemies inside us that chase away love, and my anxieties about the future which seemed more a cloudy night than moonlight, I bought sixteen peaches and cut out the stones. I placed them in a cotton bag and hammered them into shards. It took almost all my strength. Finally, I pestled the stones and kernels, covered them in brandy and left them to infuse in a large ceramic jug. In a few weeks' time I would strain this liqueur and my new friends and I would raise our glasses as we looked out at the Christmas lights threaded through the trees. This was a recipe from The Alice. B. Toklas Cook Book, which was published when she was seventy-seven. Maybe this book was a conversation with her beloved, who was now buried in Père Lachaise. Much of Stein's writing was a conversation with Toklas.

Fanny and Eva were very beloved to me. We had not so much found ourselves in Paris, as found each other. Sometimes my mother, who was long dead, returned to find me in my studio in Paris. There she is. Standing on one of my kilims, contemplating the mice. I am convinced she still knows nothing about what matters to me.

29

When Gertrude Stein was twelve, her mother, Amelia Stein, noted in her diary, 'Gertrude weighs 135 pounds.' Gertrude, in turn, wrote about her mother, or wrote back to her mother, who had died when she was fourteen:

'She was a sweet contented little woman who lived in her husband and her children, who could only know well to do middle class living, who never knew what it was her husband and her children were working out inside them and around them.'

The Making of Americans

It is a compelling assassination of a mother by her youngest child. I admire that phrase 'lived in her husband and children', as if she had no home of her own. Yes, her mother was preoccupied with making a home for her husband and children and might very well have discovered she had no place for herself in her own home. Amelia apparently had no idea what they were thinking or feeling.

In Stein's view her mother did not have the tools or the vocabulary to access what was going on inside them. She intriguingly insisted that her mother's death was a 'liberation' because she 'had little existence in her'.

Her mother was a little mother.

'The little mother was not very important to them. They were good enough children in their daily living but they were never very loving to her inside them. They had it too strongly in them to win their own freedom.'

The Making of Americans

Gertrude Stein had lost it.
What is it?
The life of her mother.
If it was a sacrificial life, she had still lost it.

What is it?
Her mother.

In her late teens Gertrude Stein was melancholy and she no longer had a little mother to measure herself against.

'. . . in those days in California I was interested in everlasting and I wondered so much about everything that I was almost alone and if you are almost alone well all that there is is almost alone.'
Everybody's Autobiography

30

Jean-Luc lived in a road near Sacré-Cœur in Montmartre. Fanny and I arrived at Métro Abbesses, the deepest station in Paris, to begin the long hike up the hill towards Rue Norvins. It was six-thirty in the evening and the cafes were crowded with people enjoying a glass of wine after work. Fanny's heels kept getting stuck in the gaps between cobblestones.

'Why are you wearing stiletto heels for this walk, Fanny?'

'For my mental health.'

'I myself prefer the curved heels of the 1600s.'

'That's because you are a king.'

I stopped to catch my breath. Sometimes I fear my heart might pack in. Why am I so breathless? Gertrude Stein is squeezing all the life out of me. We were on our way to visit Jean-Luc, uninvited, with only the most fragmentary evidence. What was the evidence that he knew more about Eva's cat than we did? His strange insistence that his walking stick would find him again as if it were inclined to make its way back to his feet of its own accord.

Was it madness to glimpse a greater meaning hiding in plain sight amongst those words? Yet, is that not what literature is for? To search the hills for greater meaning hiding in plain sight?

It is hard to know.

When Jean-Luc opened the door he was surprised to see us but did not appear to be entirely startled. In fact, he was a master of deportment. His white hair had been trimmed since our last meeting. According to Fanny, he was wearing a vintage Yves Saint Laurent suit so rare it was of immense value. The worn fabric on the elbows was on the verge of tearing. This seemed appropriate to our mission. It too had very little substance to hold it together.

'It is a pleasure to see you again.' Jean-Luc did not entirely mean it, but he invited us in and did not slam the door in our faces. I admired his courage. It was a warm and scholarly room. Book-lined. Mahogany furniture. A ceramic rooster placed in the centre of the table and next to it a chicken with wooden legs. Above the fireplace a vase stood ablaze with mimosa. One shelf was dedicated entirely to American poetry: John Ashbery, Frank O'Hara, Eileen Myles, Ted Joans, Kenneth Koch, Langston Hughes, Gertrude Stein, Barbara Guest, Nikki Giovanni, James Schuyler, Maya Angelou. Between two of the books stood a small pot of eczema-soothing moisturizer. Fanny handed him the champagne we had bought earlier, in compensation, she said, for our discourtesy at arriving unannounced. He opened the champagne gracefully and gestured to us to sit down on his leather sofa. When he was out of the room gathering glasses, Fanny nudged me and pointed to a painting on the wall.

I followed her gaze. We both saw it was the

poster that Eva had pinned to the trees on the Quai de la Tournelle.

The word LOST rendered in large letters floated above her drawing of Bob. Two red and black triangles for ears. It was not Bob as he looked, but how Eva felt him. Bob was love. Love was majestic and mischievous. And it was lost.

Jean-Luc emerged with a tray of glasses and a plate of almonds.

'They are AAAAA rated,' he said.

'No, that is the category we use for andouillettes,' Fanny replied.

'Ah.' He smiled. ' I sometimes get confused.' He gazed at me and then looked away.

'We see you have Bob with you.' Fanny sounded more accusing than she intended.

'Yes, it is irresistible. A masterpiece. Really it should win the Prix Nobel.'

He filled our glasses and asked if I was making strides with the French language.

'Her French is a murder,' Fanny informed him. 'She needs to enrol for an immersive French class.'

'But isn't the city of Paris her immersive French class? Perhaps our English friend is like André Breton when he arrived in New York in the war. He did not learn English for fear he would lose his French.'

The conversation turned to the horse-drawn carts with their rotating brushes that swept the roads of Paris in 1903. And because it was 18 November and Marcel Proust had died aged fifty-one on this date, Jean-Luc insisted we raise our glasses to toast the author.

It was comforting, he murmured, especially on a melancholy day, to remind himself that Proust understood it was grief rather than happiness that develops the power of the mind. Jean-Luc began to list, off by heart, the names of some of the boys who attended the same school as Proust, the Lycée Condorcet. Henri Bergson, Pierre Bonnard, Jean Cocteau, Serge Gainsbourg, Henri de Toulouse-Lautrec, Paul Valéry and Paul Verlaine.

It wasn't clear what we were talking about, except it was a version of lemonade and Switzerland. When Jean-Luc brought up the subject of Andy Warhol, Fanny insisted this artist definitely did not attend the Lycée Condorcet. Jean-Luc looked vaguely in my direction, but not actually at me.

'No, but he was obsessed with repetition just as Gertrude Stein was obsessed with repetition. His silk-screen prints of Marilyn Monroe were endlessly the same and endlessly different. He too was the child of immigrants.'

The conversation turned to the American dish of corn dogs. A frankfurter on a stick coated in cornmeal and then fried. It was Fanny who brought up the subject of the corn dogs.

The conversation turned to religion.

'I am Catholic,' Fanny said.

'I am an atheist who believes in transcendence,' Jean-Luc replied.

'I want it all with none of the pain.'

The conversation turned to the economy. After a while, Fanny raised her hand.

'O-kaay, with respect you both know nothing so it's pointless to hear your views on the new global order.'

Obviously the conversation turned to cheese.

'I have a preference for jalapeño in my cheese,' Jean-Luc confessed.

The conversation turned to sex.

'I believe in polyamory.' Fanny was now in her favourite neighbourhood. Arrondissement Sex.

'So do I,' Jean-Luc agreed, 'but unfortunately I can no longer have sex due to prostate problems.'

'But you have your hands.' Fanny glared at him with something like indignation.

Jean-Luc blushed. For a moment he seemed to feel dizzy. He lowered his head as if to stabilize his balance. After a while, he raised his head and asked if I believed in polyamory too.

'Oh no. I would like to hear my lover say they cherish me above all others, even if they are lying. It is my preference to be cherished rather than to be one of many.'

'Well, if I might say so, it hasn't worked out for you.' Fanny was gazing at the chicken with wooden legs.

At that moment we heard it.

'Do you own a cat, Jean-Luc?' I was beginning to sound like Chief Inspector Maigret.

'One doesn't ever own a cat.' He lowered his voice. 'Any more than I could own you.'

'But you live with a cat?'

'It lives with me.' He pursed his lips together and made shpp shpp shpp sounds.

The door opened and in padded a sleek white cat.

'Please meet Marie,' he said. 'Marie is mother of five and now quite old.'

Marie jumped with difficulty on to Fanny's lap and immediately began to sink its claws into her thighs.

'I think she's scratched off my mole.' Fanny threw the dribbling white cat to the floor.

Jean-Luc turned towards me.

'I am sorry we parted as we did. It was a misunderstanding.'

His walking stick stood erect against the bookshelf.

'Wait,' Fanny said, 'do you want me to leave?'

'Yes,' Jean-Luc said sincerely, 'I want you to leave.'

Fanny found the cigarette tucked into her belt. She opened the window and began blowing smoke gently into the 18th arrondissement.

'But what we have to talk about before you go,' Jean-Luc declared to us both now, as if addressing a seminar group of intense Hegelian scholars, 'is how Eva acquired her cat in the first place.'

'We all know that.' Fanny threw her cigarette out of the window. 'It was abandoned by the landlord of her studio, who now lives in Lyon.'

Jean-Luc lifted the plate of almonds away from Marie, who was making strange noises in her throat.

'Yet that is not exactly the truth of the matter.'

We all looked at Marie. I noticed, at the same time as Fanny, that the tip of her white tail was black and one of her ears was shorter than the other. Much shorter. The size of a human little toe. Had Jean-Luc kept one of her five kittens for himself? Was she the mother of it?

*

In the small garden of flowering Mexican orange blossom, he had told us, 'There are people and animals I miss too.'

Fanny slipped on her red-soled stilettos.

'So, Jean-Luc, what is the whole truth of the matter?'

'That is for your friend Eva to explain.'

Meanwhile, rain was falling on the dead in Père Lachaise, where Gertrude and Alice B. were buried. The time had come for me to prepare for my journey to meet them. Jean-Luc slipped his hand into the pocket of his suit jacket. When it emerged from the fraying fabric, he clenched his hand into a fist and then stretched out his palm. Lying across it was one of my hairpins.

'You lost this,' he said, 'on the night we all searched for my stolen cat.'

31

I am standing in the 33rd division of Père Lachaise in the last week of November. To find Gertrude Stein's grave I will have to walk the circular route to Division 94. I have not brought flowers or buttons or Métro tickets to place on the grave. Flowers are required to do so much of the talking. For love, for condolence, for congratulations, for apologies, for patriotism, for seduction.

That is why Stein made the rose red again in her sentence 'Rose is a rose is a rose is a rose.' 'Now listen,' she told students at the University of Chicago. 'You all have seen hundreds of poems about roses and you know in your bones that the rose is not there . . . I'm no fool, but I think that in that line the rose is red for the first time in English poetry for a hundred years.'

Eva, being a visual person, is more inspired by the saws and chisels hanging on pegs in Brancusi's studio. We agree that Stein's rose has been plucked so often it has lost its petals and thorns. And I prefer the wood shavings and stone dust on his floor to yet another anecdote about Alice B. dusting Stein's collection of Picassos. We also agree that the shish kebab and red wine Brancusi served to Anaïs Nin is preferable to the leg of roast lamb injected with orange juice that Alice B. served to Gertrude.

I am hiking in the rain in the hope that I might find it.

What is it?

An end to the torment and pleasure of Gertrude Stein.

I can't bear the pleasure.

Is Life Worth Living? This was one of the lectures that William James offered on his graduate course in psychology at Radcliffe College.

Gertrude attended his lecture and it meant a great deal to her. Here in Père Lachaise, I'm guessing that everyone lying under marble and stone asked this question too.

'The greatest use of life is to spend it on something that will outlast it,' James wrote in a letter to the Polish philosopher Wincenty Lutosławski on 13 November 1900.

In her younger years, Stein wanted to know what made life worth living. She was interested in women who suffered from nervous disorders. Perhaps she should have travelled to Vienna, pressed her finger on the bell of Professor Freud's apartment at 19 Berggasse and trained with the Freudians. After all, both Freud's and Stein's life's work would be centred on language.

'I then began again to think about the bottom nature in people, I began to get enormously interested in hearing how everybody said the same thing over and over again with infinite variations but over and over again until finally if you listened with great intensity you could hear it rise and fall and tell all that there was inside them, not so much by the actual words they said or the thoughts they had but the movement of their thoughts and words endlessly the same and endlessly different.'

'The Gradual Making of the Making of Americans', in Lectures in America

Stein disliked speaking of the past and was not interested in her own unconscious. It would have been an interesting encounter, Sigmund Freud and Gertrude Stein enjoying a cigar together in Vienna. Would Freud's wife, Martha, also referred to as Frau Professor, have made small talk with Gertrude's wife, Alice B.? Would she have exchanged her recipe for boiled beef with Alice B.'s recipe for hashish fudge? Martha Freud's favourite author was Thomas Mann, Alice B.'s favourite author was Gertrude Stein. Freud called his wife Princess when they were courting, Stein called her wife Pussy. Sigmund Freud believed that contraception caused neurosis, so after six children they refrained from sex. Perhaps Alice B. would have had something to say on this matter. Both women outlived their partners and struggled to find a way to live without the flashing lights of their genius spouses.

Freud and Stein both had a medical training and wished to do something else with that training. Stein's first ever published writing was for the Harvard Psychological Review in May 1898, titled 'Cultivated Motor Automatism: A Study of Character in Its Relation to Attention'. Freud studied at the medical school of the University of Vienna, specialized in neurology and obtained his degree in 1881. Stein studied at Johns Hopkins School of Medicine in 1897, passing anatomy, pathology, bacteriology, pharmacology and toxicology with A's and B's. Her casework had involved delivering babies in the black neighbourhoods of Baltimore, material she used for her collection of novellas, Three Lives. She failed four of her final exams because she was irrevocably discouraged by a misogynist professor.

He considered her to be a battleaxe, presumably because he felt cut down by the blade of her intelligence. Her presence. The ways in which she presented herself. Freud became the founder of the avant-garde science of the unconscious. Stein became an avant-garde writer, a leading figure in the modernist movements of her era. They both collected art. Freud acquired over two thousand ancient artefacts to expand his thinking on the ways in which the past is embedded in the unconscious present. To Carl Jung he once confided, 'I must always have an object to love.' He wanted to excavate the past of his patients and put it together to better understand how it is repeated in the present, to look back to go forward.

In one of the founding texts of psychoanalysis, Freud writes:

'Thus it came about that in this, the first full-length analysis of a hysteria undertaken by me, I arrived at a procedure which I later developed into a regular method and employed deliberately. This procedure was one of clearing away the pathogenic psychical material layer by layer, and we liked to compare it with the technique of excavating a buried city.'

Studies in Hysteria (1895) by Sigmund Freud and Joseph Breuer

And what would Freud have made of Stein? Would he have smashed into the stone (her surname means stone) and emerged with valuable treasures? Stein's pen had carefully rearranged the rubble of the buried city and the writing itself was the treasure.

'Pardon the intoning of the heavy way. Pardon the aristocrat who has not come to stay. Pardon the abuse which was begun. Pardon the yellow egg which has run. Pardon nothing yet, pardon what is wet, forget the opening now, and close the door again.'

'A Long Gay Book' (1909–11), in Matisse, Picasso, and Gertrude Stein: With Two Shorter Stories (1933) by Gertrude Stein

Stein collected modern art. She wanted to excavate the future. She was so forward-looking she never learned to reverse her Ford Model T, sent to her from America to help deliver medical supplies in France during two world wars. The dogs were usually sleeping on the back seat. Sometimes she wrote inside her Ford while it was being repaired.

There they are, Freud and Stein, preoccupied with their mutual collections of art, ancient and modern, searching for it.

What is it?

How we put ourselves together.

Gertrude Stein spoke German as a child, Freud's first language. Perhaps Sigmund would have been too much like her own father, though not as volatile as Daniel Stein. Freud's father, Jakob, was a wool merchant. Stein's father began his new life in America running a clothing store in Baltimore with his brother. If she found fathers 'depressing', Freud's female patients told him in various ways they also found fathers depressing, not least in Freud's 1905 case study 'Dora: An Analysis of a Case of Hysteria'. Dora, aged seventeen, is on the run from male predators, as is the daughter in The Making of Americans.

When Freud tells Dora that her refusal to accept his interpretation of her suffering was 'an indication of the strength of her repressed love and sexual desire for her father', she walks out of his consulting room in Vienna to take a few breaths of air in the new century. The twentieth century. Stein had walked out of her medical training one year later, in 1901. If Dora questioned the male mono subjectivity of Freud's thinking, Stein had suffered from this too at Johns Hopkins. When one professor ribaldly joked about women and childbirth, she had contested his tone and been told if she didn't like it she should leave his seminar. Her own mother had seven children, two of whom died at birth. None of this struggle is overtly aired in her writing, but perhaps it is hiding in its incoherence.

When Stein arrived in Paris to devote her new freedom to writing, aged twenty-nine, she had experienced a longer education than her supposedly more intellectual brother, Leo Stein. He had not completed any of the various degrees he signed up for at Berkeley, Johns Hopkins and Harvard. She had earned a degree in psychology, after all. All the same, Gertrude began to understand that she was required to behave like a nineteenth-century female character and lurk in the shadow of her less talented brother. She deferred to him because he was moody and fragile and he was the older brother and she was the younger sister. 'She's basically stupid and I'm basically intelligent,' Leo told anyone who would listen. Brothers can be very annoyed when they have a genius for a sister.

It is not supposed to be that way round.

The Brontë sisters understood this too. They would become famous writers and their brother, Bramwell, would become addicted to opium and alcohol. His own ambitions to become a writer and artist seem to have been thwarted. He was just not as talented as Charlotte, Emily and Ann, nor did he possess their drive and stamina. His sisters were careful not to rub his nose in their success. They might even have concealed their own success to enlarge his self-worth. If this is a special skill that girls are required to learn at a young age, things can go very wrong when they lose interest in this skill. Leo was the genius. That was how it was supposed to be. He had all the societal entitlement and encouragement and financial security he needed to succeed. Gertrude had the protection of money and all the turbulence of her gender and queerness. Leo began to ridicule her writing. He thought it was abominable. The rage of the sister and the brother. The shame of her own complicity in deferring to him must have been immense. His irritation at her sense of purpose meant she had to lose it.

What is it?
Her brother.

'Slowly and in a way it was not astonishing but slowly I was knowing that I was a genius. There was no reason for it but I was, and he was not there was a reason for it but he was not and that was the beginning of the ending and we always had been together and now we were never at all together. Little by little we never met again.'

Everybody's Autobiography

Four years after Gertrude moved in with Leo, she was going to meet the woman she called her wife, Alice Babette Toklas. Babette from the Hebrew name Elisheba. They met in the autumn of 1907. Gertrude was thirty-four, Alice was thirty. Toklas wrote in her memoir, What Is Remembered, 'It was Gertrude Stein who held my complete attention, as she did for all the many years I knew her until her death, and all these many empty ones since...'

Alice was small, dark, bourgeois, Jewish and daring. She left post-earthquake San Francisco, where she had been housekeeping for her father, brother and other male relatives since she was twenty, to get a glimpse of another sort of life in Left-Bank Paris. She travelled with Harriet Levy, her friend and neighbour. Toklas had met Gertrude's brother Michael in San Francisco when he arrived to assess the damage to some of their family properties.

In Paris, Alice B. and Harriet visited Michael Stein and his wife, Sarah Stein, at their apartment in Rue Madame to find that someone else was there.

Gertrude Stein was there, all there.

Tanned from a holiday in Tuscany.

Stein's coral brooch and her deep voice and the uninhibited way she laughed were alluring to Alice B. Here was a woman who had lost much of what she had to lose. Gertrude Stein did not try to make herself smaller or hide her intellectual capaciousness and she had devoted her life to art. She was monumental and she was also fragile. Alice B. knew that.

Gertrude invited her to visit the studio in Rue de Fleurus the next day and suggested they go for a walk afterwards in the Luxembourg Gardens. Alice B. arrived half an hour late to find Gertrude in a vile mood, shouting and stomping around. At that time, Gertrude Stein was becoming something, but she was still unpublished. Yet for some reason she felt comfortable being moody with Alice B., safe enough to be unpleasant. She instructed Alice to look at the paintings while she changed her clothes.

'I like loving. I like mostly all the ways anyone can have of having loving feeling in them. Slowly it has come to be in me that any way of being a loving one is interesting and not unpleasant to me.'

The Making of Americans

They could not legally marry, but Gertrude proposed they live their life together. Alice cried. She was deeply in love with Gertrude and soaked two handkerchiefs with her Yes. She moved into Rue de Fleurus to continue her role as erotic provocateur, intellectual companion, editor, typist, dashing cook and supervisor of their many employed cooks. Stein bought a new typewriter for her, and Leo gave up his studio so that Alice could have a bedroom. Gertrude would write by hand and drop the pages on the floor. Alice gathered them up to type out the next morning while Gertrude slept. She was intellectually excited by what she read and what she typed, protective of her lover's writing. In Alice B.'s opinion, Leo Stein could not write because he had nothing to say. Sometimes Gertrude left her love notes, signed YD. Your Darling. From Alice B.'s point of view, she had been lifted from servitude in her family home into the arms of a vibrant, witty, intelligent woman who would write her into literary history. Alice B. would not be written out, she would be written in.

There she is. Scowling in her hat.
Alice B. had lost it.
Lost what?
The obligation to smile.
Alice B. was stylish, sarcastic, clever and loving.

As the women became more involved with each other, Leo left them irritated notes about their domestic trespasses against him. It is understandable that he began to feel daily life was intolerable with his loved-up sister and her devoted partner.

*

'She is sweetly here and I am very near and that is very lovely.'

'Bundles for Them' by Gertrude Stein, in *Look at Me Now and Here I Am: Writings and Lectures 1911–1945* (1967), ed. Patricia Meyerowitz

At the same time, Gertrude was beginning to find her brother's arguments and opinions less interesting. When Leo finally moved out of 27 Rue de Fleurus it was hard for Stein to step back into a friendship with her once beloved brother. It would require her to reduce herself in his presence, to share with him none of what made her extraordinary. She would be obliged to laugh at herself, to laugh at the world laughing at her when she didn't mean it, to accept his ridicule and the ridicule of the male modernists who regarded her as an eccentric impostor on their turf. They wanted to chase her off their land and she knew it. It is recognizable, Leo's envy and his entitlement. None of this is overtly stated in Stein's poem 'How She Bowed to Her Brother', but it exists somewhere in the punctuation, in her use of full stops, which, like a needle piercing the page, are there to convey all that cannot be said.

'She did not. Bow to her brother. When she. Saw him.'

Leo and Gertrude never spoke to each other again in their lifetime. He read about her death in a newspaper. The enraged poem 'How She Bowed to Her Brother' refers to the moment she glimpsed Leo Stein in Paris traffic many years after they had ceased to speak to each other. Stein left out the pain of creating herself in her writing, her own bitterness and shame at her work being rejected and declined. She was sixty when she found big fame. It had been a long, struggling writing life.

There she is in her car. Not bowing to her brother.
 There she is in Division 94. Buried with her lover.

*

I have found the grave. A slim, modernist square of grey granite. The headstone designed by Stein's friend the artist Francis Rose. Gertrude had bought one hundred and thirty of his paintings and displayed them with the Picassos. He was flattered. They had first met when he was young, unknown, hedonistic and smoking opium in his Montmartre apartment, the room entirely painted black.

Alice B. Toklas requested that Francis Rose design Gertrude's final home, perhaps knowing that she would join her. Their names are engraved on either side of the headstone.

Gertrude Stein told us that when Alice B. Toklas was in the presence of genius, she heard bells ringing. Obviously, Alice B. heard bells when she met Stein and when she met Picasso.

I listened in.

No bells were ringing.

I could hear birds and the hum of traffic and rain falling on the trees and falling on the dead of Père Lachaise. The dead who can no longer feel the rain or suffer or search for love and fame or turn up drunk for dinner and be pushed down the stairs by their host.

Gertrude Stein.
    Naming herself a genius was a stroke of genius. Everyone would argue about it for ever.

If we create ourselves with and through language, it seems to me that Gertrude Stein's project was to dismantle herself and a whole century through language, to uncreate herself as she had been created by her father, by her sneering professor at Johns Hopkins, by her brother, to undo the manner of the nineteenth century. Get rid of commas. Get rid of question marks. She did not want to be told when to take a breath and when something was a question or who to love or how to dress. Get rid of clichés. Break through the conventions of genre. Stein was going to step out of the frame, away from the life of her mother and aunts, away from the uncomfortable femininities that had been societally constructed to keep her in her place. Her enchantment with visual art meant she was going to detour from the various modernisms of literary writers such as Pound, Eliot, Joyce and Woolf. She thought Pound smelt 'of the museum'. In Hemingway's view it was impossible for a writer to pass untouched through the storm of Pound and Joyce.

'Any poet born in this century or in the last ten years of the preceding century who can honestly say that he has not been influenced by or learned greatly from the work of Ezra Pound deserves to be pitied rather than rebuked. It is as if a prose writer born in that time should not have learned from or been influenced by James Joyce or that a traveller should pass through a great blizzard and not have felt its cold or a sandstorm and not have felt the sand and the wind. The best of Pound's writing—and it is in the CANTOS—will last as long as there is any literature.'

'Statement on Ezra Pound', in The Cantos of Ezra Pound (1933) by Ernest Hemingway

*

Gertrude Stein did pass through the blizzard and she did not feel its cold. She would make a literal home with Alice B. and another home with language. She was not interested in making it new in the way Pound wanted to make it new.

Her lucky strike was to know that she held the complete attention of someone who loved her and who was always listening. Perhaps that is what mothers are mythically supposed to do, to always love and to always listen. Yet, Alice B. was also being created again by Gertrude. Stein would rewrite them both with her pen. Alice B. had societally been written as her father's spinster daughter with no purpose in life other than to organize his home. Alice understood this act of uncreating in Gertrude's writing. They shared the same project, to be made again, to have a second life in language. The home she made with Gertrude Stein is present in much of the writing.

There she is. Walking her ghosts.
Pierre Balmain, the great couturier, used to watch Gertrude walking with her goat in the

garden of her country home. He pronounced goat as ghost.

All writing is about walking ghosts. Or perhaps the ghosts walk the writer. Towards our parents or something like them. Towards our siblings and lovers and friends or something like them. Towards the unknown. Towards the edge of a cliff.

In June 1926, Gertrude Stein accepts an invitation to give a lecture at the Cambridge Literary Club in England. The poet and critic Edith Sitwell, many rings on her fingers, draped in luscious furs, will make all the arrangements. Edith will host a party for Gertrude and Alice B. Who will be there? E. M. Forster and Virginia Woolf will be there. The Cambridge lecture is Stein's chance to defend her own work, to step into becoming a public intellectual, to lay out her stall. The years of hosting her salon and defending the outlaw artists she exhibited had prepared her for this moment. This lecture will be published by Virginia Woolf's Hogarth

Press as 'Composition as Explanation'. When she returns to Paris, she asks Alice B. to cut off her hair. Take out the pins. Cut. Cut it all off. Where are the scissors? Alice cut it to above her ears. Did she look more masculine? Or did she look more feminine? Or did she achieve brute superiority and resemble a Roman emperor? Julius Caesar. Seize her.

32

Eva had something to tell us. She is leaving Paris to join Hamish in America. Apparently, he has spent the last two years building a house for them both in Seattle. Why did she never mention the house? He had been searching for it. What is it? Land. He found it, negotiated the price, the architect had designed a floor plan they both liked, the house was now more or less complete.

Furthermore, Eva has now delivered her graphic novel to her French publishers. On the last day of November, she will be leaving her studio in the Rue des Trois Portes to sell her graphic novel to America and to live in the house that Hamish has built for her.

Fanny was furious. 'But what about us?' She

had even switched her phone to silent to ask this question. She was standing behind Eva the Fifth, who was sitting on one of the white chairs around the table in her apartment.

'Well, that is the past,' Eva said, folding her right hand into the left.

'Are you saying we are the past?' Fanny hooked her thumb on to the belt strapped across her narrow hips. 'No, Eva, we are a throuple.' Her acrylic nails were swirls of orange to which had been pasted tiny jewels.

Eva glanced at us both, as if appraising two strangers. She unscrewed the lid from the liqueur which had been infused with the peach stones and kernels and poured a large quantity into the three glasses Fanny had acquired in Verona on a romantic trip with Martine, the most obscure of her three lovers.

We knocked it back in one gulp. It was eleven in the morning.

Eva seemed to have no nostalgia or regret about leaving Paris. She poured herself another glass of the peach brandy and gazed up at me. There was a splash of red paint on her left hand.

'I think this is a recipe from Alice B.'s cookbook. Yes? Made in the wartime?'

I did not reply, merely refilled Fanny's glass and my own.

'We are moderns,' Eva said. 'We do not linger in the past.'

'O-kaay, go to America then,' Fanny replied. 'As a Danish Spanish immigrant it is likely you will be deported anyway.'

Eva told us that Hamish had confessed his life had been bleak without her.

'Yes,' Fanny was shouting now, 'but your life with us in Paris has been magnificent. Perhaps you can't bear being happier than when we found you? Look at the way you're enjoying our English friend's peach liqueur. I took you to all the clubs to dance. You devoured at least twenty of France's two hundred and thirty cheeses and all the art in our museums. We have been together through four seasons. Our English friend took you swimming. All right, swimming is not as exciting as stealing a cat, I understand, but our English friend has so generously shared her thoughts on her essay about gross Gertrude Stein with her woollen stockings and the control-freak constipated wife. I mean, Eva, you are a self-ordained assistant in this endeavour, our friend never made it official. And now you want to be alone but together with Hamish again.'

Eva shut her eyes and zoned out.

'And something else,' Fanny continued. 'Is it possible that after you arrived in Paris, you spent a lot of time making drawings near Rue Norvins in Montmartre?'

Fanny tapped the top of Eva's head. 'Bonjour, Eva. You need to check in with us on the subject of Bob.'

Perhaps Eva was time-travelling with Karl Marx to Paris in 1843 to discuss social philosophy and class antagonisms.

Eva opened her eyes and addressed us clearly and calmly.

'I have finished my graphic novel and that is what I came to Paris to complete. How do you think I earn my living? I am an artist with a commission. And now I am going to sell my novel to America and live with Hamish in the house he has built for us.'

'And what about it?' Fanny said, hands on her narrow hips.

What is it?
America. A land of immigrants.

If Bob was trying to find his way home to Montmartre, it seemed that Eva was trying to find her way back to Hamish to make a home.

'Yes,' Eva said, 'Gertrude and Alice made a stable, organized, loving home wherever they lived. Gertrude's wild writing depended on it.'

33

'And so I am an American and I have lived half my life in Paris, not the half that made me but the half in which I made what I made.'

'An American and France', in What Are Masterpieces (1940) by Gertrude Stein

My studio in Paris looks like a barn that has levitated to the top floor of a medieval building. The day before Eva left for Seattle to join Hamish, she came round to give me her white clogs and a coat she could not fit in her suitcase. Eva is not tall but she kept hitting her head on the low wooden beams. I sometimes wonder if these heavy old beams are what Balzac had in mind when he thought he might set up a business importing trees from the forests of Poland to construct sleepers for the French railways. We could just glimpse my neighbour standing on his balcony, wearing boxer shorts, his chest bared to the weather, staring at us as he spoke on his phone. Not a single bird was singing. The local boulangerie had a long queue of tourists waiting to buy the croissants that had once won a prize in 2018. 'And how will you spend the holidays?' Eva wanted to know.

'I will return to London,' I told her.

'What is happening in London?'

'Why, my London life,' I replied. 'And when I return to Paris in January I will buy a galette des rois filled with frangipane at our boulangerie. This I will share with my neighbours and let their children find the lucky charm hidden inside it.'

Now that Eva owned a house of her own she obviously thought she could advise me on how to put together my studio. I suddenly understood why she trimmed her fringe all the time. Eva wanted her life to be a straight, symmetrical line.

'These kilims must go. They cover everything.

The tiles under the rugs are something to celebrate not to conceal. And you are all covered up too. Look at your fur hat. No wonder you have mice. There are so many places for them to hide.'

She rummaged around in her tote bag for a while.

'I have prepared some essential oil of peppermint for you,' she said. On the front of the tote was a sentence from one of her graphic novels. The tote was merchandise. I began to realize that Eva was very organized and commercially successful. 'So about this peppermint oil.' She had at last found a small glass bottle at the bottom of her tote. 'Mice don't like the smell. It confuses the ways they communicate with each other, so they find somewhere else to live.' She started to sprinkle my kelims with her peppermint mixture, and then stopped to point at the two sprigs of rosemary perched on the shelf above my fireplace. It was Eva who had given them to me when she first arrived in Paris. 'It's an effective herb for inflammation,' she had told me. I was still not sure what it was in Eva that was so inflamed, but I wanted to find out and knew I would write about it when I had the time. The white clogs she had placed on the floor looked strangely spectral, as if her body had already been spirited away.

Eva's studio on the Rue des Trois Portes had become our headquarters. She was skilled at making a home of her own and welcoming friends and strangers to it. It was warm in winter, cool in summer, loving in every season. Tomorrow she would close its three doors and return the key to the landlord's agent. After a while, she looked at the time on her phone. Fanny was coming over to her place to sit on her suitcase so she could close it. And Fanny, like Picasso, was always punctual. It was raining, of course. I looked for my spare umbrella to give to her. It had disappeared under one of the suitcases stacked by the front door. I was pleased that Eva knew nothing about me except for our life together in the continuous present. I had friends who had known my mother, my father, my sisters and brothers, they had known me at fourteen and at thirty and onwards. It was something of a relief to exist in the continuous present tense from Monday to Sunday.

A mouse ran across the room and started to frolic on the kilims.

It turned to look at us both. It almost waved. It seemed to love the peppermint oil.

'So Gertrude Stein made a life in France and you will be making a life in America,' I said to Eva.

'Yes,' she replied. 'That's what modernism is all about. How we put ourselves together.'

Eva touched the ends of her fringe, which she had trimmed that morning.

'I am off to make the American part of my life.'

'Goodbye, Eva,' I said. 'I will miss you and I don't think I will ever write my essay on Gertrude Stein.'

'Yes,' she replied, 'and given you are flirting with a snow leopard and fighting with mice, I will write it for you. I reckon the title will be My Year in Paris with Gertrude Stein, but as it will mostly be about the anguish of preparing to make my way to Seattle, I might call it

My Year in Paris with Gertrude Stein

The Making of an American.' She gripped the umbrella I had passed to her and kissed me on both cheeks. 'Gertrude Stein was a big presence, but I don't think anyone can ever get to the bottom of it.'

34

'And identity is funny being yourself is funny as you are never yourself to yourself except as you remember yourself and then of course you do not believe yourself.'
  Everybody's Autobiography